PENGUIN BOOKS

Sons For The Return Home

Albert Wendt was born in Western Samoa and is a member of the Aiga Sa-Tuala. He studied for twelve years in New Zealand, at New Plymouth Boys' High School, Ardmore Teachers' College, and Victoria University, Wellington, where he gained an M.A. in History. In 1965 he returned to Western Samoa to teach and soon afterwards became Principal of Samoa College. In 1974 he joined the staff of the University of the South Pacific, and is now the Professor of Pacific Literature. In 1986 he was the Foundation Visiting Professor in Pacific Literature at the University of Auckland.

Albert Wendt has written three novels, *Sons for the Return Home*, *Pouliuli* and *Leaves of the Banyan Tree*, which won the New Zealand Wattie Book of the Year Award in 1980; two collections of short stories, *Flying-Fox in a Freedom Tree* and *The Birth and Death of the Miracle Man*; and two volumes of poetry, *Inside Us the Dead* and *Shaman of Visions*.

Sons For The Return Home

Albert Wendt

PENGUIN BOOKS

Penguin Books (N.Z.) Ltd, 182–190 Wairau Road,
Auckland 10, New Zealand

Penguin Books Ltd, Harmondsworth,
Middlesex, England

Penguin Books, 40 West 23rd Street,
New York, N.Y. 10010, U.S.A.

Penguin Books Australia Ltd, Ringwood,
Victoria, Australia

Penguin Books Canada Limited, 2801 John Street,
Markham, Ontario, Canada L3R 1B4

First published by Longman Paul 1973
Published in Penguin Books 1987

Copyright© Albert Wendt 1973

All rights reserved

Printed in Hong Kong

No part of this publication may be reproduced,
stored in or introduced into a retrieval system, or
transmitted in any form or by any means,
electronic, mechanical, photocopying, recording,
or otherwise, without the prior written permission
of the publisher.

*In memory of my brother Lloyd,
who could not make the return*

PART I

1

He was bored with the lecture. He got up quietly, picked up his books, left the lecture hall through the back door and went to the student cafeteria.

It was lunchtime. Almost all the tables were occupied. He put his books on a vacant table near the large windows overlooking the harbour. He waited nearly thirty minutes (so he noticed on the cafeteria clock) in the queue at the counter before he was able to buy a meat pie and a cup of coffee.

When he got back to his table he found a girl sitting in one of the chairs. She was writing on a pad and didn't pay him any attention. He sat down. (He preferred eating alone.) He started eating and soon forgot the girl. It had rained nearly all that morning. The window-pane was blistered with raindrops; he watched them as they slid, like peeling strips of skin, down the glass. The dark heads of the trees immediately below the windows nodded noiselessly in the wind. He suddenly felt the girl watching him. He continued staring at the window and sipping his coffee. She stretched her left hand forward as if to touch his arm but abruptly withdrew it when he glanced at her. He looked at the window again. A passenger liner was ploughing a thin furrow of foam across the dark blue waters of the harbour, heading for the entrance. From that distance and height it looked like a toy ship.

'Do you mind me sitting here?' she asked. He shook his head without looking at her. 'You don't talk much, do you?' He continued to ignore her.

She sat very quietly for a while, gazing at the window and tapping the pen she was holding in her left hand on the cover of the pad in front of her; then, more uncertain, she asked if he was studying at university. He maintained his silence. 'Is there something wrong with me?' she asked.

'No,' he said, still not looking at her.

'You want to be left alone, is that it?' she asked. He nodded. She picked up her pad and got up. He waited for her to go, but for a moment she just stood looking down at him. He glanced up at her. She shoved the pad under her left arm and stalked off, her high-heeled shoes clicking across the tiled floor.

He looked down at the harbour. The liner was disappearing through the harbour entrance; it rose and fell in the swell of the open sea. He gazed up at the Rimutaka Range across the harbour and saw a wall of storm clouds shifting ponderously down towards Eastbourne and the harbour. He got up and left the cafeteria to catch the cable car down to the city and home before the rain could start again.

That night, while studying in his room, he remembered the girl. She was attractive, blonde, and wore no makeup. Like a model out of a fashion magazine, he thought. He wondered if he would ever see her again.

His mother brought him a mug of hot cocoa at eleven thirty. She sat on his bed and talked to him in Samoan while he drank the cocoa. He nodded and mumbled something now and then. She was a big woman, and the voluminous woollen dressing gown which she wore made her appear even larger, more formidable. Half an hour later she told him not to study too hard and to go to bed early, and then left his room.

He got into his bed when he heard his older, bus-driver brother, who had been working the night shift, enter the house, and his mother came out of her bedroom to get him his supper.

As he lay gazing into the darkness he found himself thinking of the girl. At the cafeteria she had been no more than an annoying presence but now he was experiencing an inexplicable desire to see her again.

Just before he toppled into the calm pit of sleep, he heard a renewed surge of rain hitting the roof of the house. The sound reminded him of the patter of rats' feet.

2

Their first morning at sea the boy screamed and clung to
his mother when they ventured from their cabin. His father
tried to soothe him with caresses and whispered
affirmations that there was nothing to be afraid of. The boy
screamed louder. Some of the other passengers and crew
gathered to see what was wrong. The sight and smell of all
those strange white people speaking a language he didn't
understand only frightened him more. His parents
retreated with him into the small cabin.

His mother sang him to sleep, but he woke and clung to
her, trying to shut all his senses to the throbbing of the
ship's engines, the nauseating odour of diesel, and the sight
and feel of the strange beds and furniture in the cabin.

That afternoon his parents persuaded a Samoan passenger who could speak English to ask one of the stewards
to bring their meals to the cabin. For the rest of the
journey, which took six days, they rarely left their cabin.
In the evening, when there were no people on the decks,
the man and the woman would go out and enjoy the cool
refreshing breeze and salt spray while the boy slept.

One night after their evening service — a hymn, a
recitation of the twenty-third psalm, and a prayer — the
man went to the upper deck alone because the boy was
awake and the woman had to stay with him.

He strolled warily up towards the stern of the ship, past
the noisy dining room and bar. He met no one. He stopped
at the railing. The sky and the sea were calm and armoured
with moonlight. Stars were scattered across the heavens.

The man felt unafraid for the first time, and he thought longingly of the islands they had left. In the moonlight the mast above the ship's holds glittered like a cross. To his left lay a row of lifeboats covered with oil-stained canvas.

The man turned and peered at the lifeboats when he heard the weird, muffled moaning. In the shadows under the nearest lifeboat he saw two figures in a tight embrace. They would see him if he moved so he remained where he was. The moaning, soft at first, grew louder. Someone gasped and he saw the figures break apart. One of them rolled out from under the lifeboat; the moonlight caught his face as he zipped up his fly. It was the steward who brought them their meals. He stood up, brushed back his long hair, and motioned to his companion to come out. From under the lifeboat emerged another man, one of the crew. The steward embraced him, they kissed quickly, and then went off towards the other side of the ship. A wave of vertigo hit the man. He turned and fled back down into the cabin.

He vomited into the sink. His son woke up because of the noise and started sobbing again. He went over and told him to be quiet. The boy wept softly into his pillow. The woman woke and the man told her what he had seen. She clung to him and cried.

They never again walked the decks; they remained in the cabin for the rest of the voyage.

As the ship drew closer to New Zealand it grew colder. The man and the woman were afraid to ask the steward for more blankets. The woman slept with the boy in her bunk and gave her blankets to her husband.

Just before the ship docked in Wellington, the woman dressed the boy in a grey sweater, shorts, long socks, and shoes. The man reluctantly put on the brown suit which his brother had sent him from New Zealand. While the man and the boy stood in front of the full-length mirror, trying awkwardly to adjust to the strange clothes they would have to wear in the new land, the woman got dressed. The boy started whimpering, pleading with his mother to take off the shoes which were hurting his feet. She calmed him with promises of ice cream.

They were the last passengers to go down the gangway.

They emerged from the ship into the cold air of New Zealand, clutching one another's hands and peering fearfully at the crowd on the wharf. A crew member poked the man in the back, urging him to move on. The woman picked up the boy and followed her husband down to the solidity of the wharf. The man searched the crowd for a familiar face. He saw his brother waving to him from behind the customs fence and he felt less afraid.

The man looked back at the ship before getting into the taxi with his brother. Wharf workers were already starting to unload its cargo of bananas. He asked his son to look back. The boy refused. The man put an arm round his wife's trembling shoulders. She too didn't want to look back at the ship. We've arrived, he whispered to her, God has been kind; He will continue to protect us. He saw tears in her eyes. He remembered the two men making love under the lifeboat, and got into the taxi quickly.

The woman handed him the boy. He held on to his son tightly, as if by protecting him he too would be protected in the years they would have to spend in this alien country.

The man started work with his brother at a factory the next day. Ten months later they shifted from their relations' home to a flat in Newtown. The boy's older brother came over from Samoa at the end of their first year in New Zealand.

3

He bought some sandwiches and a glass of milk and went towards his usual table by the windows. He saw the girl and was turning to go when she stood up and waved to him. He thought of ignoring her, but he was curious, so he went and sat down opposite her, with his back to the windows. He started eating. She looked down at her arms folded on the table. He noticed that she wore seven silver bracelets on her left wrist.

'Don't you believe in conversation?' she asked, smiling at him.

'Sometimes,' he said.

'And you can smile,' she said.

They found themselves laughing easily. They talked. She did most of the talking. Whenever their eyes met she attempted to hide her interest in him by looking down at her arms. She told him that she was the spoilt daughter of a businessman. He asked him jokingly which business. She told him, and added that her father was stingy with money. She asked him about his studies. He told her he was finishing a B.A. in history. Very boring, he told her. She explained that she had started a science course the previous year, but had dropped it because she found it uninteresting and she wanted to be a fashion model. Her father had argued her into continuing at university. Since he was paying for it, she had agreed to study English.

He gave her a sandwich. While she ate she continued talking about herself. He noticed that she had very unusual blue-green eyes and a mole on her cheek. She wore a platinum ring, shaped like a snake, on the middle finger of her left hand. Her nail polish was the colour of finely polished steel.

'What about you?' she asked suddenly. He shrugged his shoulders and didn't answer. 'Well, tell me about yourself,' she insisted.

'I'm Samoan,' he said. He watched her closely.

'I thought you were a Maori.'

'There's very little difference,' he said.

'Suppose not,' she replied.

She glanced at her watch and sprang up. 'Got to go to a lecture. Can I see you again?' He nodded. 'How about taking me to the pictures tonight?' He agreed to meet her in front of one of the theatres that evening. 'You pay, okay?' she asked jokingly.

He watched her as she moved through the crowded cafeteria. She stopped near the main entrance and talked and laughed with three men at one of the tables. One man patted her familiarly on her buttocks. She laughed as she went out the door. He felt jealous.

On his way home that afternoon he realised that she was the first girl — the first papalagi girl — he had ever really enjoyed being with for nearly two years, since he had stopped having an affair with one of the librarians in the main city library.

Her leg rubbed against his, like a warm snake. He glanced over at her. In the dim light he could see her smiling at him. She reached over, grasped his hand, and held it in her lap and caressed his fingers as if she was smoothing down the ruffled feathers of a frightened bird.

All the way through the film, a John Wayne western which he didn't really enjoy, she laughed and clapped and sometimes stamped her feet on the wooden floor. He wanted to tell her not to be so noisy but didn't. The people near her got annoyed, and the bald man directly in front of them turned round and told her to act her age. She ignored him.

'The old bastard can go and get shoved,' she whispered.

9

'I thought you liked westerns,' she said to him when they came out of the theatre. He didn't know what to say. Holding on to his left arm and nuzzling her cheek into his shoulder, she added, 'I don't really like westerns either. Just John Wayne. He's got no acting ability. I like people who aren't able at anything. You know why?' He remained silent. ''Cause I ain't got talent either,' she said, imitating John Wayne.

As they moved down the street under the cold blazing lights of the shops, she asked him, 'Are you talented?'

'At what?'

'At writing poetry, or something like that.'

He shook his head. She laughed and he laughed with her. 'Liar!'

'But why?'

'You are talented!'

'But at what?'

She stopped walking and, gazing steadily up at him and trying not to laugh, said. 'In the use of silence.' He continued walking. She ran to catch up to him.

'What's the matter? Have I said anything wrong?' she asked. He shook his head. She pressed her face into his shoulder. 'I'm sorry,' she said.

The crowds thinned out as they neared the railway station. She was to catch the unit to Lower Hutt where she lived with her parents. He realised that he was trying not to like her.

They stopped at the pedestrian crossing opposite the station. A red taxi screeched to a halt in front of them. Its back door was pushed open and a man was shoved out on to the footpath. The taxi roared off again. She rushed to the inert figure and knelt down beside it.

'He's bleeding!' she called to him. He went to her and pulled her to her feet. 'But we must help him,' she insisted.

'He's just drunk.' He steered her round the man on the ground and across the road.

On the other side she looked back. When she realised he wasn't going to help, she pushed him away, hurried up the station steps, and disappeared into the depths of the building.

He got a taxi home so he wouldn't have to see the unconscious man on the footpath.

4

He was a school prefect and in the upper sixth form. He was also a member of the First Fifteen — the first Samoan to be chosen.

He was only a fourth former when he was first picked for the team. The girls of the school suddenly took an interest in him, and he lost his virginity one night after a school dance, behind the gymnasium under the eucalyptus trees. It was quick, clean, almost meaningless for him.

The girl, who had since left school, led him into the darkness. Quickly she unzipped and clutched him, kneading his waking penis with frantic hands. With her skirt hiked up to her hips she fell upon him. The next day she boasted about it to other girls, but he managed to avoid them for the rest of that year. The following year, as his reputation as a player increased, he discovered he couldn't avoid them any more. Not that he wanted to in the end. To stop them from possessing him, he made love to them as that girl had used him. During the day he acted as though he didn't know them.

He restricted his trust to the three other Samoan students in the school. He didn't even bother to accept as friends the other members of the team once they were off the rugby field.

In the classroom he studied conscientiously, said little, and did well. At first he was proud of being called (and treated as) 'the best Samoan student our school has ever had'.

One morning, after he had passed School Certificate, the Principal called him to his office. He found his parents in the room. The Principal told him to sit down beside them. He noticed that his parents were smiling that obsequious smile they reserved for papalagi. He immediately felt ashamed and angry.

'I've just been telling your parents that our school is very proud of you,' the Principal said. 'But I don't think they understood me. Do — do they speak English?'

'Not very much, sir,' he mumbled.

'Well, tell them that I'm really proud of you. You're the first Samoan to pass School Certificate in this school.'

He told his parents hurriedly. They thanked the Principal in Samoan oratory.

'What did they say?' the Principal asked him. He told him. 'Your whole race should be proud of this boy,' the Principal said to his parents just before they left.

That night when he got home from school he asked his parents not to visit the school again. His mother cried and inquired why; his father got angry and threatened to beat him if he didn't act civilised.

'Because they humiliate you,' he said to his mother. 'We've been here for nearly thirteen years and they still treat us as strangers. As inferiors.'

'But they don't treat you that way,' his father said. 'Look at how they've helped you get where you are!'

'Only because they can't do anything else, Papa. I'm better than them at that stupid game they worship so much. I can compete with the best of them in class as well. I speak their language, their peculiar brand of English, as well as any of them. They have to pretend I'm their equal, that I'm a New Zealander, because they can't do anything else.'

'They don't!' his mother insisted.

He was almost crying. 'Mamma, have you forgotten all the humiliations we've had to suffer since we've been here? Have you forgotten how they treated my brother? He only spent a year at that school and he wanted to leave. They called him a 'dirty coconut Islander', and when he beat up the kids who called him that, the Principal — the same condescending man who refused to call you by your names today — caned him in front of the whole school and called him "a brainless Islander who should be deported back to the Islands". Have you forgotten that?'

His parents said nothing for a long time. Their older son came in and sat down near the woman. The smallness of the room, the oppressive heat of the electric heater in the fireplace, and the ceiling lights seemed to knit them together inseparably, completely self-contained.

'You are proud of being Samoans?' their mother asked them. They nodded. 'Never forget that,' she emphasised.

'Must say you two play at being papalagi extremely well,' their father said.

'We try,' his older son replied, smiling.

Over dinner that night they joked and laughed about what had happened.

'We're all going back home as soon as he finishes university,' their mother said, pointing at her younger son.

'Deported back to Samoa?' her husband said jokingly.

'Where else? The South Pole?' she said.

It was half time in the game. The score was three all. He was sitting on the ground with the rest of the team, listening to their coach outlining the mistakes they had made and how to correct them. The coach asked him if he had anything to add. He shook his head; he knew they could win the game; he could win it for them. He had calculated how to break past the second-five marking him; he only needed to make the move when the time was right in the second half and the championship would be theirs.

The seats on the terraces were packed with spectators, but he was only interested in seeing where his parents were. He stood up and surveyed the crowd. From high up on the eastern terraces echoed the ringing sound of a warrior's whoop. He waved and the group of Samoans up there cheered and waved back. 'Kill them, coconut!' he heard his brother call from among the group. He laughed and waved.

Some parents had come on to the field to give oranges to the team. He didn't accept any. He waited. When he saw his father coming across the field he ran to him. He knew that his father was feeling uncomfortably small with the papalagi crowd watching, so he embraced him, acknowledging to all of them that he was proud of this small shy man.

His father handed him a peeled orange. He ate it quickly.

'What shall I do?' he asked. His father was dressed in a stained gaberdine overcoat much too big for him. At one time he had been ashamed of the way his father dressed; he had thought that it made it obvious to papalagi that they were not New Zealanders, just unsophisticated immigrants from the islands.

'What do you mean?' his father asked.

'Do you want me to win the game for them?'

Looking gently at him, his father said, 'You are old enough now to decide for yourself.'

The game was nearly over; the score was still even. The crowd was shouting in abandonment. The ball wasn't coming out of the lineouts and scrums cleanly. He had to have the ball. While a lineout was being formed, he called to their halfback that they had to have the ball.

Their wing threw in the ball, the ruck formed, and he saw the ball coming out on their side. The halfback dive passed it out to the first-five, and then it was in his hands and he was making his move. He sidestepped to his left; his opposing number hesitated and tried to tackle him as he shot off to his right and was through the gap and out to his left again, running for the corner flag. He glimpsed the fullback running towards him from his right.

He had to decide.

He chose to win the game; play it their way; they could not harm him.

The newspapers predicted that he could develop into one of the finest players in the country and become the first Samoan to be picked for the All Blacks.

He refused to play after he enrolled at university the following year.

5

Mind if I sit down?

No.

Why didn't you help that man? Was it because you didn't want to get involved with the police?

Yes, but not just the police.

Who then?

With anyone. You get involved if you help people. Or hate them.

Or love them.

Yes. Or love them.

But what about your parents?

I am involved with them. But only them and my own people.

Then you do feel something for someone.

Yes.

What about all those other two-legged creatures outside your chosen circle?

Would you like a sandwich?

What about those other people?

They can take care of themselves.

Is it because most of them are white — pakeha?

That has something to do with it.

Racist.

True. Very true. They turned me into one.

God, how you must despise me. I'm pakeha, in case you're colour-blind. What an idiot I am. Here I am throwing myself at you and all the time you're laughing at me!

I'm not laughing at you.

Then you must despise me?

No.

Then what?

What do you mean?

What do you feel about me?

I just don't want to get involved, that's all.

Then it's goodbye, man. Enjoy your self-righteous detachment. By the way, here's my phone number just in case you want to abuse some pakeha bitch over the phone.

He didn't ring her for five days, and he didn't go to the cafeteria. On Saturday night, after getting drunk with his brother at a friend's flat, he rang her from a phone booth and told her he liked her but he didn't want to ever see her again.

Two days later, on his way home from university, he met a woman on the crowded bus. She rubbed her belly against his flanks as they stood in the aisle, holding on to the ceiling straps. He followed her out of the bus to her dingy room.

The woman locked the door behind him. The walls of the room were covered with numerous photographs of her. Some showed her nude and much younger. She stood in the middle of the room and started undressing. He noticed that she wasn't looking at him but into a full-length mirror on the wall in front of her. She examined her profile, then her hands and shoulders, all the while crooning softly to herself. She took off her bra and, caressing her sagging breasts, white like stale milk in the light, she closed her eyes, and her hips moved back and forth almost imperceptibly. 'Aren't they beautiful?' she murmured, holding up her breasts.

He started towards her. She motioned to him to stop where he was. She slid off her pants and, gazing into the mirror, caressed her hips and flanks and between her legs. 'Wouldn't you love to do me?' she moaned.

She tried to move away as he came and pulled her into his arms and pushed her up against the mirror. 'You love

pakeha women, don't you, boy? Don't you?' She stank of
dried sweat, and her thick makeup was flaking off her face
to reveal wrinkles, pimple scars, and a network of bluish
veins.

Her flesh felt flabby and cold against him as he made
love to her.

He found himself thinking of the girl.

Where have you been? I've been looking for you everywhere. Even tried to find your address. No one in the
university seems to know.

Been around.

Where?

Trying to forget you.

Did you succeed?

Did you want me to succeed?

No.

I didn't. I even made love to another woman to try and
find out whether I — whether I liked you.

And what did you find out?

I like you. And I do want to get involved.

By the way, who was she?

Who?

The other woman?

Just someone I met.

Did you enjoy it? Never mind, don't answer that
question if you don't want to.

I felt sorry for her.

Before or after?

All the time.

Was she pakeha?

Yes.

But I thought you didn't want to feel sorry for us pink
people!

6

After her late English lecture they walked out of the central building into the evening which had risen from the harbour as though it had been born out of the sea's depths. He held her hand and they talked softly as they walked.

Gnarled pine trees guarded the steep eastern entrance to the university grounds. Under them lay old, moss-stained graves — remnants of pioneer settlement. At university, whenever he wanted solitude, he sat on one of the graves and gazed down at the city, at the houses and buildings, which reminded him of mausoleums and which rolled away from under him in rows of terraces.

The air was warm and smelt of rain. It was the beginning of summer.

Her hand trembled in his; he held it protectively and it grew still. They stopped under one of the pine trees. He embraced her, bent down and kissed her for the first time. She held him tightly.

'I want you to make love to me,' she murmured into his neck. 'Now.'

They moved into the shadows under the pines. He spread out his duffle coat on one of the graves. Before he embraced her again, he smelt the odour of pine sap and damp earth in the air. 'Hold me,' she whispered, shivering as if she was cold.

They lay down on the warm lid of the grave. The pine trees hummed above them.

Afterwards she told him that he was very good. He got up and started picking up his duffle coat. 'I'm sorry,' she said. She stood up and buried her face in his chest. 'I didn't mean to sound so clinical. I suppose it's my very pakeha way of trying to tell you I feel a lot for you.'

She straightened her clothes. He gave her satchel to her, and with arms wound round each other they went down towards the inner labyrinths of the city.

She told him that many men had made love to her. How many? he asked. She couldn't remember. Ten? he said. About eight. Why did you have to tell me about it? he said, trying to free his arm from round her. You asked me. They walked in silence for a while.

'Did you enjoy it with them?' he asked.

'I wouldn't have made love to them if I hadn't enjoyed it.'

'Did you really enjoy it with me?'

'I told you I did,' she said. He pushed her away and continued walking alone.

'You want me to lie to you? Tell you I didn't enjoy it with the others? Is that it?' She gripped his arm and turned him round. She wound her arms round his waist, her belly thrust up firmly against his thighs, and gazing up into his face, she said: 'I don't want to ever lie to you.'

7

The party was well under way when they arrived. The sitting room was crowded, rock music shook the room, and a few couples were dancing in the middle of the floor. He had been to only a few student parties before; he avoided them. He usually attended parties held by young Samoans; he went with his brother who seemed to know every Saturday where all the parties were.

She pulled him into the room and left him by the door. He noted the easy familiarity with which she went round greeting many of the people, mainly students. She kissed a few of the men.

Returning with a glass of beer for him, she asked if he was enjoying himself and then went off again to join a group of people round the gramophone at the other end of the room. He wished his brother was there, someone familiar he could feel comfortable with. He drank his beer quickly.

An effeminate young man sat on the settee in front of him, talking shrilly to three girls. To his left, leaning against the wall, were five youths dressed in scruffy jeans and sweaters; two of them had scraggly beards and one wore sunglasses. The youths stood silently watching the dancing couples. Now and then one of them refilled their glasses with beer poured from a flagon. All round the room lay, stood, and crouched a horde of students, most of whom he didn't know. He noticed one of his history lecturers among them. The man was surrounded by six students; he seemed to be delivering one of his lectures. Opening the bottle of whisky he had brought with him, he started to drink from it. Cigarette smoke swirled lazily up to the ceiling where it shifted from wall to wall, unable to escape from the room. He hoped she would return to him soon and make him feel part of the party and the world she could move through so easily and from which he had deliberately ostracised himself.

Half an hour later she came and took him over to meet her friends by the gramophone. She introduced him; he just nodded. They tried to engage him in a conversation about Samoan politics. He didn't say much so they continued talking among themselves. He went on drinking the whisky. She asked him again if he was enjoying the party. He nodded and tried to smile.

'You're not really,' she said laughingly. He insisted he was enjoying it. She got them two glasses from somewhere. He half filled her glass. She told him to fill it to the brim. She nestled into his side and he put his arm round her. They watched the people dancing.

'So this is where you learnt to be so detached and good at analysing people,' she said. 'Why don't you join in? It's much more fun. By the way, have you noticed how those other scheming females have been watching you all night?' She laughed when he automatically looked round the room. 'Come on, let's dance before one of them puts her claws into you.' He told her he wasn't a good dancer. 'All Islanders are supposed to be terrific dancers,' she said. She immediately noticed her mistake and apologised. He took her hand and led her into the middle of the room.

As they danced, she called to him to stop being so shy and tense. Relax, she said. He hadn't danced for a long time but, watching how happy and graceful she was, he forgot the others and eased gradually into the flow of the music.

She kissed him as they came back to their drinks. She said bottoms up. They drank until their glasses were empty. Where did you learn to drink like that? he asked. From my old man, she said with a laugh.

He admitted to himself that this was the happiest time he had ever spent in New Zealand. By loving her, he was feeling for the first time a growing and meaningful attachment to the country which had bred her. He kissed her. Someone tapped him on the shoulder.

'Want a dance?' said a male voice over his shoulder. He turned. It was one of the bearded students he had seen earlier. The student ignored him and asked again.

'Is it all right?' she asked him.

'Are you with him?' the student said, still not looking at him.

'Yes, I am,' she replied.

'Okay, if that's the way you want it.'

'That's the way I want it,' she said.

The student turned to go. 'Bitch!' he mumbled.

She grabbed his arm as he started reaching out for the student. He tried to relax again. 'Thank you,' she whispered. 'Do you want to go now?' He nodded.

They left.

They had come in her mother's car. As they drove away he looked out the window, trying to hide his shameful anger from her.

'Now I'm beginning to understand what it's like,' she said. She reached over and gripped his right hand.

The starless sky seemed to press down on the car as it rushed headlong into the neon lights of the city, pursuing tram rails that glittered like knife blades.

I love you.
I love you too.

8

One of the main city rubbish dumps lay three streets behind the boys' home. Originally the rubbish dump had been a large gully with a creek flowing through it. Now the gully was half filled with refuse, high mounds which looked like gigantic anthills. During summer, when the rubbish decayed quickly in the heat and rain, the stench permeated the whole neighbourhood. The older boy discovered the dump first and took the younger brother there two weeks later, on a Friday afternoon. They collected soft-drink bottles — six dozen of them, washed them in the brown syrupy water of the creek, which still continued to ooze out from under the mounds of rubbish, and sold them to a bottle dealer. They continued to visit the dump every Friday afternoon whenever they had nothing else to do after school.

Out of discarded tins, cardboard boxes, twisted pieces of metal, hulks of cars and refrigerators, tattered clothes and shoes, broken furniture — in fact out of the discarded, useless ends of the city, the boys constructed castles, houses, and roads: a miniature city which belonged totally to them. They destroyed their city before leaving for home in the late afternoon, only to reconstruct it in a different pattern the following week.

They sometimes caught rats, lizards, and butterflies and locked them in the crude miniature houses. When they returned the following Friday they usually found them gone. One time they found that two of the rats had died. They conducted a mock burial service, built a small funeral pyre out of some dry boxes, wrapped up the shrivelled corpses in newspaper, placed the bodies on the pyre, and set it aflame. They pretended to cry, like some adults they had seen at real funerals, as the bodies burnt in the crackling flames.

Whenever they found other people foraging in the dump, they hid and observed them.

One old man, carrying a large sack and riding an ancient bicycle, started coming regularly every Friday. He usually arrived just as the boys were getting ready to leave.

The first time the old man came, the boys lay on top of one of the mounds and watched every move he made. It was their first opportunity to observe a papalagi adult that close up.

The old man had long fluffy white hair (like a small cloud, the older boy said), rheumy eyes, and sunken cheeks; and dried saliva collected at the corners of his wrinkled mouth. He was emaciated and was stooped forward permanently from the waist up. His black suit was threadbare and patched in many places. He locked his bicycle and stood it against the hulk of a car near the road. He then made his way up the first precarious mound, carefully gaining footholds in the rubbish. The various parts of his body moved in a series of emphasised jerks as if he was a puppet.

Reaching the top of the mound, he took out a ragged handkerchief, wiped his hands first, then his face. In the sunlight and set up against the blue sky, he looked like a scarecrow the boys had seen in one of their school books. They giggled when he nearly stumbled forward and down the other side of the mound.

As the old man disappeared over the top, having stirred up colonies of flies to take flight round the first mound, the boys crept stealthily up to the top and lay down and watched him. He paused every few yards, dislodging tins and other rubbish which rolled down before him into the creek, took out his handkerchief, and wiped his hands and face. The boys were puzzled by the handkerchief ritual because as yet he hadn't touched any rubbish.

26

The old man reached the creek and knelt down and washed his hands. For the next hour or so he just sat on a box and gazed into the water. He remained perfectly still; it was as if he was frozen. The boys grew impatient. The older one hurled a small rock down into the creek. The old man jerked up to his feet.

'Don' shoot, please!' he cried. The boys giggled and dug each other in the ribs. For a moment the old man shook as he looked all about him. Then he shut his eyes and seemed to sigh.

For the remainder of the afternoon the old man wandered all over the mound near the creek. He picked up nothing. He merely turned up with his foot whatever caught his interest, bent down and peered at it, smiled, nodded, and moved on. Flies swirled around him but he didn't seem to notice.

The boys went home puzzled.

The old man went through the same ritual the following Fridays.

A month later, just before Christmas, the boys hurried to the dump to collect bottles to sell. From the road they heard the old man shouting something they could not understand; he sounded as if he was in pain. There was not a breath of wind and the stench was stronger. The boys scrambled up the first mound, sometimes slipping and getting their feet cut and bruised and their clothes soggy with mud and decay.

From the top of the mound they saw that the old man was surrounded by six boys. They were laughing and jeering at him. One of them rushed forward when the old man wasn't looking, jabbed a fist into his back, and ran back to close the circle they had formed around him. The others laughed and danced up and down. The old man whimpered and tried to break the circle by hitting at the boys with his empty sack.

The boys on the mound didn't know what to do. They had grown to like the old man, but he was a papalagi and his tormentors were papalagi too. They lay and watched.

From that height, the boys below looked like a pack of rats attacking a helpless animal.

The torture continued until the old man crumpled to his knees, pressed the sack against his face, and wept. 'Don', please!' he cried, rocking back and forth on his knees. His tormentors just laughed. One of them rushed forward and wrenched the sack out of the old man's hands. 'No! No!' cried the old man, crawling on his knees after the boy. 'It mine. Gimme, please!' The boys whistled and clapped. Then the boy holding the sack flicked it like a whip against the old man's face. The old man crossed his arms over his face and head and sobbed.

'Dirty foreigner!' the leader of the group shouted. The others started chanting the same thing as they danced round the old man.

'Leave me alon', please!'

The leader stepped forward and kicked the old man in the back, and he toppled forward on to his face. The others jabbed kicks into his sides.

The boys on the mound left the safety of its summit and, picking up two rusty steel rods, moved down cautiously. The others heard them and turned. The leader stepped forward, saw the steel rods and stopped.

'Leave the old man alone,' the younger brother warned him. (He spoke better English than his brother.) The other boys formed a threatening line beside their leader.

'What are you dirty Islanders going to do about it?' the leader asked. The older brother swung the rod threateningly close to the leader's stomach. The line jumped back. The brothers moved forward, swinging the rods before them. The line retreated slowly. 'Dirty black bastards!' the leader shouted. The rod, swung by the younger brother, caught him a numbing blow on the right hip. He held back a painful yelp and, clutching his hip, scrambled back out of range. The line broke apart immediately.

The two brothers stood protectively above the old man and watched his tormentors scattering up and over the nearest mound.

'Fucken coconuts. Go back to where you bloody well came from!' one of them shouted.

The old man was whimpering into his hands. Reaching down, the older boy patted him gently on the shoulder. 'No, please,' the old man whined, cringing closer to the ground, without looking up.

'It's all right now,' the younger boy said. The old man lifted his head warily and peered up at them from under crossed arms. The boys smiled at him. The old man hugged his face with his hands and shouted:

'Leave me alon'!'

Puzzled, the boys looked at each other.

'It's all right,' the younger boy repeated. His brother reached down to the old man to help him up. The old man screamed and slapped his hands away.

'Don' touch me! Ya — ya dirty Nazis!'

The boys edged away.

They didn't speak to each other all the way home, each nursing his own pain in silence.

On Monday morning the younger boy told his teacher about the old man, leaving out what had happened the previous Friday afternoon. He can't speak English properly, he added. Probably a foreigner from Europe, and he sounds slightly insane, his teacher said.

'What is *foreigner*?' he asked her. He knew already but he wanted an answer from her, a salve to soothe the pain now lodged in his core like an ulcer.

'Oh, someone who comes from another country,' she replied.

Never again did the boys go to the rubbish dump. Never again to construct, destroy, and reconstruct their fabulous city.

Nazis? What is Nazis?

9

Like most other Samoan families in Wellington, their lives
revolved round the Pacific Islanders church. This was why
they had shifted to Newtown: it was closer to the church.
After a few years the man was appointed a deacon, his
younger son — in his final year at high school — taught
Sunday school, and his wife became a respected member
of the church social committee. They attended church
twice on Sunday and rarely missed the Wednesday prayer
meetings and the socials on Saturday nights.

The Sunday morning the man was ordained deacon he
remembered his father and thought about him on their way
home after the service.

His father had been well known for his healing skills. He
came from an ancient line of healers. He could set broken
limbs, massage away all sorts of internal pain, lance boils
and carbuncles and abscesses, and heal cuts, wounds, yaws,
and sores using herbal mixtures. But most of the villagers
were frightened of him because he could also cure illnesses
and diseases caused by ghosts and evil spirits. They
invested him with supernatural powers and referred to him
as a pagan, a fearful reminder of the times before the
missionaries arrived in the islands. The pastor and the
village elders refused to make him a deacon. In public they
condemned all belief in ghosts and evil spirits; but when
someone in their families fell ill and they could find no
natural causes for the illness, they took the patient to him.

Their home, which consisted of three fale, was situated
at the western end of the village and set up against thick

groves of palms. Most of the villagers planted coconut palms in straight lines and therefore were amused by the man's eccentric way of planting. Every year at the start of the rainy season, he and his four sons cleared a few acres of virgin bush and planted three new groves. Each grove consisted of thirty palm saplings planted in a circle of about thirty yards in diameter. No one knew why, not even his youngest son, who — ashamed of the other children teasing him about his father's groves — asked him repeatedly for the reason. They look beautiful that way, he'd say. Or, it's a good way of ensuring that storms won't blow them down. This was only one of his father's many strange ways.

Sometimes he would say nothing to anyone for weeks on end. He would withdraw into a circle of impregnable silence and emerge from it only when he chose to. Once in the circle he seemed utterly self-contained. He would go alone into the mountains and bush, and after a few days return laden with strange plants, roots, and leaves. He would chew them or cut them up, wrap them in ti leaves, and store them away in the pandanus basket he kept under the only bed they had.

Some nights he would just sit by the lamp and gaze out into the darkness as if he was expecting someone. Other nights he would vanish into the palm groves, and in the silence of the dark they would hear him chanting unintelligible incantations. At the end of his vigil, just before dawn, they would hear the frightening sound of a conch shell being blown three times.

When he decided to join his family again, he would laugh and play with his sons, take them fishing, and on Sunday go to church with his wife. He usually slept through the service.

The first patient the man had seen his father cure was a girl who had been suddenly and mysteriously taken ill. Her family brought her to him at night so that the pastor would not notice. They told him that she was possessed by an evil spirit. He instructed them to leave the fale, and got his sons to pull down the fale blinds and light the lamp.

The girl lay swathed in blankets near the lamp. Now and then she would shudder uncontrollably and try to struggle out of the blankets. He held her down and told his youngest son to sit by her head and keep her down by pressing on her shoulders. He told the rest of his family to leave the fale.

The boy grew frightened. Beads of sweat glistened on the girl's twitching face, and saliva dripped from the corners of her mouth. Her eyes rolled round in their sockets and she stank of urine. But he held her down every time she struggled.

His father got a small bundle of herbs and a bottle of coconut oil from under the bed and came and sat down by the girl. He chanted an incantation which the boy didn't understand, and waved his right hand in a strange circular manner over her face. Then he opened the bundle of herbs, poured some coconut oil into it, mixed it with his fingers, and started rubbing the herbs over her cold forehead and then gradually down over her face, all the time reciting the incantation in a whining voice. As the boy watched the caressing movement of his father's hands and listened to the chant, he grew unafraid. The girl relaxed gradually. The boy noticed that she had shut her eyes and was breathing easily.

Shortly after, the girl began to speak in a strange male voice. Frightened again the boy looked at his father. He told him there was nothing to be afraid of. It was only the illness leaving her. The girl continued to utter phrases which meant nothing to the boy, as the man's hands massaged her neck and shoulders gently. An hour later, after he had massaged her breasts and belly, the girl was sleeping peacefully.

Four years or so later, after the boy had seen his father heal many other cases of this type, he finally asked him about them. His father told him that there were no such beings as ghosts or evil spirits — only fear and ignorance. From that day his father began to teach him the skills and knowledge he had inherited. In every generation it is always the youngest sons in our family who must carry on, his father told him. They have always proved to be the most gifted.

His father died suddenly six months later. He was buried in the middle of the most ancient of the palm groves.

Nearly thirty years afterwards his youngest son migrated to New Zealand.

'What's the matter?' the man's younger son asked him as they walked home from church.

'I was thinking of your grandfather.'

'Sure wish I had known him,' said his son.

'I never really knew him either,' he had to say finally. 'Only that he was a good man.' He pondered for a moment and then added, 'He was a healer.'

'A pagan, you mean,' said his wife, laughing. 'He'd probably turn in his grave if he knew you were a deacon in a Christian church.'

'He didn't have time to teach me,' he said, more to himself than to the others.

'Teach you what?' asked his son.

'How to get a degree at university,' his mother said jokingly. Her son laughed with her, but the man remained silent, his head bowed as if he was searching for something on the footpath.

10

After a few weeks she suggested that he should meet her parents. He asked her why. Because they want to meet you, she said, laughing. He avoided giving her a definite answer until the seventh time she asked him. Then he said to leave it until they had finished their final examinations.

In November, after they knew that they had passed all their subjects, she reminded him of his promise. He told her to arrange a time and a place. You sound as if you're getting ready for a diplomatic conference, she said. He tried to smile. She told him not to look so glum and terrified; her parents weren't all that formidable. She kissed him. Anyway, if her parents didn't like him, he always had her to have 'conferences' with! When was he going to introduce her to his parents, she asked. Whenever she wanted to, he said. How about Christmas, she said. He shrugged his shoulders. They arranged for her to pick him up on Friday evening and take him to Lower Hutt to dinner. He asked if anyone else would be there. Just her parents, she said.

His brother trimmed his hair on Thursday night and teased him about being frightened of meeting a rich businessman and his rich business wife. He attempted to joke back but he found he couldn't. He was scared, he admitted to himself. His brother reminded him of how Samson lost his strength when Delilah gave him a crew cut. They laughed about that. He instructed his brother not to tell their parents where he was going. As yet they didn't know about the girl and how he felt about her.

As he was dressing on Friday evening, his mother entered his room and asked him where he was going. To the pictures, he lied. In your best suit? she asked, smiling. Yes, in my best and only suit, he said, trying to distract her. I thought you hated suits, she said. And since when have you liked having haircuts? He told her he was a new man. She sat down on his bed, and in critical silence watched him dressing. When are you going to start attending church again? she asked suddenly. He ignored her question.

When he finished dressing she straightened his tie and the lapels of his suit, retied one of his shoes, and asked him to turn to the right and then to the left while she examined his appearance. Since when have men started using perfume? she asked. It's not perfume, he said; it's shaving lotion. Oh, she said. So tell me who this girl is, she said. Just a girl, he replied, turning to leave. A Samoan girl? she asked. But he was out the door.

His brother winked at him when he entered the sitting room. His father looked up from the TV and whistled. What lucky girl is going to enjoy your beautiful silence tonight? his father said jokingly. He just smiled and said he would be back late. Since when did one man have to ask another man if he could go out and enjoy a woman's company, his father said with a laugh. Since the introduction of tapered suits from Italy, his brother improved on the joke. So he's Italian, is he? said his father. No, said his brother, just a plain Samoan villager imported to New Zealand from the bush districts!

He could still hear them laughing as he opened the front gate.

She kissed him when he got into the car. You know something? she asked. He shook his head. I love you, she whispered.

All the way out to Lower Hutt, the car purring easily as it raced along the motorway, she caressed his thigh and kept reassuring him that everything would go well. Let's stop the car and make love, she suggested unexpectedly. In the middle of this lordly highway? he said. Why not? she said, trying not to laugh. 'Cause it ain't moral and your innocent, law-abiding parents won't like it, he said, laughing. She grabbed between his legs. He jerked away in mock fright. She laughed. Just wait until I get you later on, she said.

He grew tense again when they turned off the motorway.

The large ultra-modern house was brightly lit; it looked like a ship stranded on the side of the hills. All around it stood a wild profusion of native trees. As they approached it up the steep narrow road, he smelt the pungent odour of newly cut grass and crushed leaves.

It was a spacious sitting room, designed and furnished like a room in a modern fashion magazine. Bright wall-paper, deeply varnished cabinets and low tables, a long white settee, plush armchairs, sheepskin rugs on the floor, expensive ornaments and figurines and paintings on the walls. Everything glittered in the light of four lamps set round the room.

She introduced him to her father. They shook hands and the man inquired if he wanted a drink. He asked for a beer. The man went to get it. She grasped his hand, told him to relax, and went off to help her mother in the kitchen. He recognised two of the pictures on the far wall — prints of paintings by Gauguin of Tahitian women.

The man handed him his beer and asked him to sit down. He took the armchair opposite his host. They avoided each other's eyes. The man shook his glass of whisky; the ice tinkled.

'How long have you been here?' the man asked. He told him. 'So you've seen a lot of the country?'

He shook his head. 'Not really. Just a bit of the North Island.' His glass was empty. The man went to get him another drink. He noticed that the man walked with a slight limp.

'So you've had most of your education here?' the man asked. He named the high school he had attended and said what he was studying at university. 'I did an accounting

36

degree myself,' the man said. 'Good whisky. Want to try some?' He refused politely. The man got him another beer.

'I've been to some of the islands,' the man said. 'Been to Fiji but mainly on business trips. New Caledonia, Tahiti — really good there, even though it's bloody expensive. Never been to Samoa. I hear it's a beautiful place.' The man got himself another whisky and put a large bottle of beer on the table beside his guest.

They drank in awkward silence. The man chuckled unexpectedly and said, 'Hell, I don't know why we're so formal with each other. Do you?'

'No,' he said, laughing softly.

'Drink up!' the man said. 'You know, the worst bloody place I've been in — and I can't avoid the place because of business — is Australia. You been there?' He shook his head. 'The Aussies are the rudest, most uncouth bastards I've ever met. They get carried away with the virile surfie image. . . .' The man went on talking about Australia for a while. He felt at ease listening to him.

The girl came in. He got up to go with her but her father said, 'C'mon, honey. Let him be. We're just beginning to enjoy each other's company.'

'You mean — you're just starting to enjoy the grog,' she said jokingly. Her father laughed. 'Mummy wants to meet him.' She took him into the dining room.

'Hurry back!' her father called.

She was a small woman, nervous behind thick spectacles. He shook her limp hand. The girl asked him if he liked fillet steak, butter beans, sliced tomatoes, and potato chips. He nodded. Tweaking him playfully under the chin, she said, You better like them — that's all you're getting for dinner. She disappeared into the kitchen.

He didn't know what to say to the woman. She turned and went round the table, straightening the cutlery.

'Beautiful home you have here,' he said.

'Thank you,' she said, looking up. When he didn't say anything else, she went on straightening the table. Then she saw that his glass was empty. She took it and went to the sitting room to refill it.

He could hear her talking to her husband. He suspected they were talking about him, but he didn't mind at all. The man had made him feel at home, with his open honesty. But what was there about the woman that made him feel sorry for her?

The man did most of the talking at the dinner table. His wife picked at her food, spoke occasionally, and withdrew again into her fragile silence. Sitting opposite their guest, the girl would wink at him now and again without her parents noticing. He tried his best to concentrate on what the man was saying. He talked mainly about his war experiences. He had been a bomber pilot, had got shot down over Germany two years before the war ended, had been shot in the leg while trying to escape from prison camp, had spent the remainder of the war in the camp. As the man talked of the war his voice shook with excitement.

The man finished eating and asked his wife to bring him a bottle of whisky. He drank heavily as he talked. His wife and daughter seemed used to it. The girl occasionally attempted to divert his attention from the war by telling him that their guest was getting bored, but he ignored her. He described in dramatic detail how the bombs were released from the belly of the plane; and how, from the air popping with flak, he would watch them explode in silence, and buildings and streets disintegrate in a frenzy of smoke and fire; and how he would imagine the people down there scurrying round screaming and dying. War was completely senseless, the man said.

He suddenly didn't want to listen any more to the man's horrific stories. He couldn't divorce his attention from the woman and her brittle sadness. At first he had thought she was acting like that because of his presence in the house. But the cause was deeper, older than that. He accepted another glass of wine from the girl. She smiled at him and he felt her foot rubbing against his leg. Its reassuring warmth distracted his attention from the others. He placed his right foot between her feet and moved it slowly up towards her knees, caressing the insides of her trembling legs. She pretended nothing was happening.

The man said he had to go to a meeting. The young man saw the girl glance at her mother. The woman tried to smile. The man nearly stumbled backwards when he got up. His wife rose to steady him. He moved away and said he was quite all right.

Near the door he turned slowly, peered at the young man, and said, 'I'm happy to have met you.' He straightened up; his face was red and he looked quite drunk. 'I'm happy for my daughter.'

Soon after, the woman excused herself and went into the kitchen.

'You know why they got married?' she asked, clutching the steering wheel of the car. He put a comforting arm round her shoulders. 'They got hitched because of me. He returned from the war, met her, got her pregnant.' He cradled her into his side. She cried softly as he caressed her hair and face.

Below them lay the city and suburbs of Lower Hutt, a shimmering expanse of lights twinkling in the gloom. Beyond that, the dark harbour, and, billowing up to the dim sky, the hills of Wellington, glittering like gigantic Christmas trees which had fallen over.

'Are your parents unhappy together?' she asked after a while. The darkness shifted lazily outside the car.

'Sometimes,' he said.

'But they love each other, don't they?'

'I think so.'

'How can two people live together year after year, slowly destroying each other? I've often wanted to tell them to get a bloody divorce, tell them I'm sorry for having got them married.'

'Why haven't you?'

'Because they won't do it. Can hate be a kind of love, do you think? ... I prefer the quarrels, but those awful silences, sometimes whole weeks of it — slow silent torture!' She arched her head over his arm resting on the back of the car seat.

They sat in silence for a long time. The city below them burned.

'I sometimes want to leave them, go and live on my own, but I can't. I love them in my own funny way. And mother's only got me. You know why I brought you home tonight?' He didn't reply. 'Because I wanted you to see what we can become.' She pushed her face into his neck. 'Why does he talk about the war all the time?'

'Perhaps it was the only time he was ever truly alive. And happy. Like my father.'

'Was he in the war too?'

'No. But he was truly happy and alive in Samoa. I suppose my mother is the same way too. Our whole life here is only a preparation for the grand return to our homeland. Their hopes and dreams all revolve round our return.'

'And you?'

'I don't know any more,' he said.

'But why not?'

'Because you're here.'

She held him tightly. 'Make love to me!' she cried. 'Love me!'

Did you come?

Yes.

Was it good?

Yes. Yes. Yes.

Were all the others pakeha?

Others?

You know?

Yes. Why do you keep asking me about them?

Oh nothing.

Love me?

Yes.

11

The coconut palm groves and the plantation of taro and bananas provided adequate food for the whole family. The men spent a few hours each day tending the crops. Every year, just before the rainy season, they cleared new land and planted more crops. They went fishing perhaps twice a week and brought home mullet, bonito, shark, and octopus. The women fished the reef for shellfish and crabs. They also kept a middling-sized herd of pigs and some chickens. Sometimes they sold copra and dried cocoa beans to the village store and used the money to buy salt, flour, sugar, tinned meat and fish, kerosene, and cotton material to make clothes. They gave any surplus money to the church and other village projects or used it to travel into Apia, the only town. All their meals were cooked in one communal kitchen fale. Every evening they ate together in the main family fale which their father had built years before.

The youngest brother got a wife and lived with her in a small fale which his brothers helped him to build. His older brothers and their wives and children also had separate fale. Soon after their father died, the second oldest brother went to live in Apia; he worked as a bulldozer driver and rarely visited the village. He married, and a few years later returned to tell them that he was migrating to New Zealand. They dried copra and cocoa and sold it to help pay his fare.

Alone he went to New Zealand. Some months later he sent for his wife and three children. He wrote letters to his family in Samoa, telling them how easy life was in New Zealand — good pay, good schools for the children, and the Samoan church was the fastest growing church in the new land. Sometimes, usually just before Christmas, he sent them large sums of money. He bought a house and then wrote and asked the rest of the family to shift to New Zealand. He suggested that one of the older men should come over first, work, and send money back for the next one to come over, and so on. The two oldest brothers didn't want to go; they insisted that the youngest should go because he had no children. The youngest didn't see any need to migrate, he was satisfied with what he had; he was also afraid of going to an alien land of ice, snow, and cold winds which blew in from the Pole. So their brother's request was forgotten for a time.

Like most other couples in the village, the youngest brother and the woman had simply eloped and started living together as husband and wife. They met one night when he went to her village with a concert party. They eloped that same night without her family knowing. His family woke in the morning to see her cooking their meal.

After two years they were still without children. People he knew started joking about it to him. Get another wife who will give you sons, his oldest brother advised him. He considered it seriously for a while, and mentioned it to her. She wept and told him she would return to her people if he wanted her to. He realised then that he needed her more than he wanted sons to give proof of his manhood, and he told her he didn't want her ever to leave him. God will give us children, he said. Three months later, while he was visiting another village with a group of elders, he made love to another woman. At the end of the year a man he knew from that village told him that the woman had given birth to a daughter. His wife heard about it too but said nothing to him.

An old woman of their family advised his wife to consult a traditional midwife two villages away. On the pretext of visiting her family, she went. The midwife examined her, rubbed herbs over her belly, and instructed her in new ways of making love to her husband. She also gave her a packet of scrapings from the bark of a certain tree. She was to soak the scrapings in water and drink the liquid each evening before sleeping with her husband. It didn't work. In desperation she told her husband what she had done. He sent her to see traditional healers he had heard his father talk about. One of them advised her to consult a papalagi doctor in the town hospital.

Most villagers distrusted papalagi medicine and cures. Many fearful stories were told of how patients were injected with mysterious liquids which bloated their bodies until they died agonising deaths; of how wounds were stitched with sinnet which rotted in them so that the patient died slowly, his limbs decaying one by one; of how papalagi doctors used babies and corpses to experiment with, cutting them apart with saws, and feeding the parts into devilish machines; of how the doctors just peered into a patient's insides, using strange mirrors and implements, and then had him strapped on to a table under blazing lights, and cut open with sharp knives. Such stories circulated wildly every time someone died on the operating table.

Finally they decided to go to the hospital. (She had never been to the hospital as a patient; and he had only visited sick friends or relatives a few times.)

A nurse told them to wait outside the consulting room. Other people came and waited on the benches behind them. No one said anything. There was a strange smell in the waiting room. (He had heard people of his village talking about it — the smell of death, someone had remarked.) He started to feel nauseated.

The door into the consulting room opened. Another nurse, immaculately ominous in her starched white uniform, came out and called his wife's name. His wife looked at him, he nodded to her. She went slowly to the nurse, who steered her into the room and closed the door.

Soon after he hurried out of the waiting room and vomited into an open drain behind the building.

On the way home in the last bus they avoided talking about what had taken place in the doctor's office. He was too afraid to ask her in case his suspicions and fears were confirmed.

Lying under their mosquito net that night, after everyone else had gone to sleep, she told him.

The doctor was a young man, pale like the underside of fish. He had brown spots all over his face and the back of his hands, and his hair was the colour of fire. He frightened her at first. But, as he talked and the nurse interpreted what he said, she grew less afraid. He asked her about her monthly illness and how often it came. She felt embarrassed as she told him. (Men should not discuss such things, should they? she asked her husband.) Then the nurse took her behind a curtain and told her to undress. She didn't want to, but the nurse insisted and said that the doctor was only trying to find out why she couldn't have children. Didn't she want a child. She undressed and the nurse gave her a gown to wear. She lay down on the bed behind the curtain. Then the doctor came, she whispered to her husband, turning her back to him. He clutched her shoulder and said, And? When the doctor and the nurse came, she turned her face away so that they could not see the shame she was feeling.

The doctor pulled open the top of her gown. She felt something cold on her chest above her breasts. She looked up quickly. The doctor was wearing a strange rubber instrument which stuck to his ears. He was holding the mouth of the instrument to her chest and seemed to be listening to her heart beating. The nurse whispered to her to uncover her breasts, and the doctor continued to place the mouth of the instrument all over her chest. Please don't ask me to tell you the rest, she said to her husband. Tell me, he commanded. Did he *touch* you? She nodded her head. I will kill him, he said. She rolled swiftly into his arms and said, it was not the way you are thinking; he did touch me with his hand, but only to examine me so that we may be able to have a child. He pushed her away.

A flying fox squealed from the tops of the mango trees beside the fale, and the dumb roar of the surf beat into the still dark. I do want a child, your child, a son, to prove I am a woman and your wife, she said. I believe the papalagi doctor will find the cause of my barrenness. He is a good man. He is my last hope.

He held her. And mine too, he whispered.

She visited the doctor once a week for a month. She made the forty-mile trip every Friday morning on the bus. She had the operation the following month. All the elders of her family waited outside the operating theatre; some of them prayed. A year later she was pregnant. His family did not want her to have the child in the hospital. The child will die, they told him. He went and asked the doctor if he would deliver the baby personally. The doctor said that he would.

They named the baby after that papalagi doctor.

Two years later their second son was born.

He wanted his sons to have a good education, as good as the papalagi doctor's. They tried to save money so they could send them to a school in Apia, but it was always spent on one family affair or another — weddings, funerals, donations to the church.

When his younger son turned five and was ready to begin school, he wrote to his brother in New Zealand. He would forsake for a time the land that he knew, understood, and loved so that his sons could acquire the miraculous knowledge that wonderful doctor had possessed.

What is ice and snow?

I don't know. We'll find out when we get to the new land.

What are papalagi people like?

If they are like the doctor who delivered you, they are a good people.

Why is it that their skins are so white?

God created them that way. Now don't ask any more questions. Go to sleep.

Is God a papalagi?

12

Every summer he worked for three months during the
university vacation. He used the money to help pay his
tuition fees for the following year. His father and brother
paid the rest and gave him spending money whenever he
needed it. So when university ended in November he
started working as a postman. A degreed man as a
postman? his father asked. (He had completed his B.A.)
Why not? he said. Why don't you work in an office or
something like that? his mother said. Why work at all?
said his father. We have more than enough money to put
you through university next year. Because I want to work,
he said, and this time I want to work as a postman.

At the post office they gave him a dark green uniform.
It was made of thick prickly wool and it looked like a
military uniform. He didn't like it, so when he began his
round the first day he wore only the trousers and left the
jacket and cap at home. He had to cover a block of streets
in one of the older suburbs which extended over a group
of hills near the centre of the city. He enjoyed climbing the
winding streets, the mail bag heavy on his back. The
morning was bright, clear, and warm. He finished
delivering the mail in two hours, went home, and slept. He
got up in the afternoon and went to the post office to return
the empty mail bag. He met the girl that night and she
asked to go with him the next day.

She came in her mother's car and they collected the mail
bag from the post office. They drove to his area and parked
the car at the beginning of the first street.

'This is pakeha reservation country,' he said, sweeping his arm over the houses, and hills. 'The natives are quiet, eagerly awaiting the arrival of the black missionary bringing them epistles from Rome, Corinth, and Timbuctoo, spicy moral pornography from Cathay, sermons from the wild hill country of Disneyland, telegrams of death from Hine-nui-te-Po of the enormous womb and the grinding thighs!'

'Who was she?' she asked.

'The Maori Death-Goddess,' he said, with a laugh. 'I think she looked like you. Only she was "coloured", as the natives in this reservation would say.' She punched him lightly in the stomach. 'Slave-woman with the hair of fire and the thighs of milk, pick up that bag!' he commanded.

She snapped to attention, saluted him, and groaned as she pretended to lift up the heavy mail bag.

'Told you you were good at nothing else but massaging my back,' he whispered in her ear. She slapped him on the cheek. He grabbed at her belly. She jumped away and laughed.

'Not here, massa,' she said. 'What will the natives think?'

He put an arm through the shoulder straps of the mail bag and hauled it on to his back. 'Onward, missionaries!' he shouted and marched off up the street. She laughed and watched him.

It had rained in the early morning. The sun was playing lyrical tunes of flashing light on the damp walls and roofs of the houses and the surface of the road and footpath. He turned and watched her running up towards him. The sparkling light swam up from the road and footpath and made her hair look as if it was burning. She wore only a tight short-sleeved blouse and jeans; her bare feet danced through the streams of light on the footpath as she ran.

He pulled her into his arms and pushed his face into her hair.

'Is anything wrong?' she asked.

'I don't want to ever lose you,' he whispered.

'It's all right, honey,' she reassured him.

47

The first house had a fat mail box attached to the top of the front fence. It had a hole for magazines and newspapers, and a slot with a flexible metal flap over it for letters.

He handed her two letters and said: 'Madam, would you be gracious enough to slide these pearls into this kind woman's eager slot?'

'By all means, sir.' And she slid the letters into the mail box.

'No laughter is permitted in this reservation!' he cautioned her. Straightening up, she tried not to laugh.

They moved up to the next house. 'Now, Madam, this sermon wrapped in gold leaf is to be presented to this bald-headed gentleman.' He handed her a magazine rolled in brown paper. 'Madam, please ease it musically into this gentleman's hole.' She bowed to him and slowly slid the magazine into the hole in the mail box. 'Thank you, Madam.'

'Any time, sir,' she said. 'The gentleman seems to love sermons delivered that way.'

The next house was set well back from the road behind tall trees. It had immaculate lawns, orderly flower beds, and a wide driveway. 'The people of this house are poor, Your Highness, and deserve no favours from your beautiful hands,' he said.

'Yes, but can't I give them a few coins to keep them loyal?'

'If that is your wish, Madam.' He gave her a thick bundle of letters and bills, and sighed.

'Is that all?' she asked, looking at the bundle.

'Yes, Madam, our Chancellor of the Exchequer has informed me that our kingdom is nearly bankrupt, so we cannot afford to spend money on the ungrateful poor. These are just a few trifles to warn them that the bubonic plague is rife in Newtown and will soon arrive here to bloat their foul bellies and limbs and thereby provide fodder for the rodents.'

Instead of putting the letters through the mail slot, she wrenched open the back flap and stuffed them into the box.

'There. Such creatures do not deserve coins through their shrivelled slots or spineless holes but through their toothless gobs!'

'Excellent, Madam.'

Further up the street stood a small decrepit house. It had a broken-down front fence, the lawn was unkempt, and rubbish lay all over it. The mail box, broken from its bolts on the fence, was perched on one of the fence posts.

'Now here, Madam, is a rich and important lady. She deserves all the pleasure of your hands and gracious words.'

'Yes, she really does look like a member of the aristocracy who deserves my attention and gifts.' She caressed the top of mail box. He gave her a propaganda leaflet.

'Here, gentle lady,' she said to the mail box, 'accept this rather meagre and catholic gift which has come all the way from the bourgeoisie of the U.S.S.R. Peruse it carefully for hidden messages of love and remember to use it sparingly once in the morning, once at noon, and once at night.' She dropped the leaflet into the box.

The next mail box was in the shape of two miniature houses, exact replicas of the house behind the fence.

'Now what do we have here, sir?' she asked.

He peered at the miniature houses. 'Two rather foppish gentlemen. Madam,' he said. 'They seem to be holding hands.' Putting his mouth to her ear, he whispered, 'I think they are in love.'

'Oh,' she said, stepping away from the mail box. 'Oh, dear. What is our godly, one-flag, one-queen country coming to!'

'It must be the immoral influence of that religious game some of those debauched Polynesian savages introduced into our kingdom centuries ago, Madam.'

'Game? Religious game?'

'Yes, Your Highness, I think it's called the Double-Backed, Four-Legged, One-Stick Dancing Game.'

'Never heard of it, sir.'

'Never, Madam?'

'Never. Is it an intellectually stimulating game?'

49

'It involves all the senses, Madam. And doctors recommend it for all the organs of our frail bodies.'

'Where can I find a suitable instructor?'

'I do not want to sound boastful, Madam, but I am quite competent at the game.'

'Good. You may start teaching me as soon as this boring tour is over.'

'By all means, Your Milk-Breasted, Vice-Thighed, Honey-Mouthed Highness!'

She flung her arms round him and the street rang with their laughter. There was a flutter of wings in the nearby bushes, and some sparrows burst up into the air and scattered away over the roof tops. A spotted dog scrambled out of the next house and started barking at them. Still laughing, they ran to the other side of the street.

'Come on,' she said laughingly. 'Let's fill all these slots and holes with delicious messages from the Two-Backed Monster, and drive to a quiet place where you can teach me and teach me and teach me that beautiful game!'

It took them an hour to deliver the rest of the mail. They drove to one of the secluded bays, made love on the sand between rock outcrops, and then swam in the chilly waters of the harbour.

She accompanied him every day on his mail round. Afterwards they went to the movies or swam. And they made love. Living totally within each other's laughter and warmth and flesh, as summer flowered towards Christmas.

A week before Christmas, when the main streets of the city were peopled with plastic and papier mâché Santas and reindeer and angels dancing mechanically to the monotonous tunes of Christmas, he was fired. An old woman caught them making love in the alleyway between her house and the next one, recognised his uniform, and rang the post office. Get slotted! the girl laughed at the old woman as they ran away. The old woman rang the post office again.

The personnel officer sent for him that afternoon and told him that the post office had had enough of irresponsible Islanders and Maoris who, instead of working,

would rather seduce innocent girls or do nothing all day
long. He controlled his anger and asked for his pay. Just
before leaving he told the personnel officer that he had
enjoyed missionising for the government, bringing
laughter and joy and life to frustrated slots and holes. He
wished the red-faced man a jolly, weapon-sharpening
Christmas and left, slamming the door behind him.

The girl was waiting for him in the coffee bar opposite
the post office. Imitating the personnel officer's speech and
gestures, he told her what had happened. They laughed
about it.

'What are you going to do now?' she asked.

'You mean, what are we going to do for the rest of this
glorious vacation,' he said.

'Okay, ex-postie. What are *we* going to do?'

'Each other, I hope,' he whispered. She slapped his
shoulder.

'Why don't we just get a car and explore this
godforsaken island?' she said. 'Why don't we? You know,
just fly and make warm juicy nests all over this land? I can
borrow my uncle's van. We have camping gear at home.
I'll show you what New Zealand's really like. Have you
seen much of it?'

'No, but I'd like to, especially with such a proficient
guide,' he said, reaching out under the table and caressing
her legs.

'Be serious. Would you like to?'

'Okay, but after Christmas.'

'Why after Christmas?'

'I've never missed spending Christmas with my parents.
Would you like to spend Christmas with us?'

'I'd love to. And you did promise to introduce me to your
parents.'

'We'll hit the long road the day after Christmas. Okay?'

He remembered as they left the coffee bar. 'What are
you going to tell your parents?'

'About what?'

'About our trip.'

'Oh, that I'm going with some girlfriends.'

'Won't they find out?'

'It doesn't matter. They know I'm capable of defending my long-lost honour. What are you going to tell your mummy and daddy?'

'Oh, that I'm going with some girlfriends!'

'No orgies are permitted in this heavenly kingdom of ours,' she said. 'One God, One Queen, One Country. Blow permissive Maoris and Islanders; we'll bring them out to perform dances for our VIPs and then crucify them to Technicolor posters where they rightfully belong!' He wanted to tell her not to talk so loudly in public but he suddenly found himself chanting: 'Up with the RSA, Anzac Day, the All Blacks, the TAB, and the affluent proletariat. Marx wasn't born in a manger. We found him in a golden cowshed using a milking machine on the contented national cow.'

'To the wall with Mao, Uncle Ho, and the Vietcong! Shave Guevara's beard!'

As they marched up the main street to the car they went on chanting improvised slogans. Some people stopped and stared and shook their heads. Others moved warily out of their way. A few told them to act their age. Up you! the girl and the young man gestured with their hands.

Christmas sang in the heart of the city. And he felt at home in it for the first time in his life.

> *Postie, postie, come today,*
> *bring me a letter from faraway.*
> *Postie, postie, come today,*
> *let my dog bite you until you fray.*

13

During the man's first four weeks in the factory he worked at odd jobs — swept the floors, helped out in the cafeteria, and oiled the machines. He was afraid of the factory; he understood little of what went on in it. Caught in the noise, the overwhelming size of the building, the intricate system of machines and conveyor belts and cables, the large number of workers whose language he didn't understand, he felt small, lost. It was as if he was trapped in the belly of a huge metallic fish, he told his wife when he came home from work the second day. He felt safe in the fish only at morning-tea time and in the lunch hour when he was with the other Samoan workers. He told his wife that his job was not fit for a man: girls and old men could do it. He yearned to work with crops again; to get up in the morning and go into the plantation and watch the earth in flower; to feel the pulse of green life in the leaves of taro and yam. Or to go out to sea to fish, and be healed by the silence of the sea's ever-changing mystery. He was not used to the monotonous routine of getting up early in the morning, catching a crowded bus, and filling in a certain number of hours with humiliating work. But he enjoyed the big pay he received at the end of every week; it was more money than he had ever earned before. He saved most of it so he could pay for his elder son to come from Samoa.

One evening he asked his brother to explain what the factory was all about. The factory manufactured thousands of tins and other metal containers, his brother said. About three hundred people worked there. Every worker had a definite job to perform in the complex chain: if one worker did not do his job properly, the quality of all the work would deteriorate. The factory, his brother went on, was owned by a very wealthy family. You ought to feel privileged to work in such a well-known, wealthy organisation, his brother added. But when am I going to get a better job? he asked. In this country, his brother explained, you have to be patient and work hard, and you will be promoted. Look at me, said his brother. I've worked hard and look where I am now. Only ten years and I'm in charge of one of the biggest machines. Many papalagi have worked for nearly twenty years and not been given control of such a machine. He had to admit that his brother was indeed an important man in the factory. Why don't you ask your foreman friend to get me a more suitable job? he asked his brother.

At the end of the month his brother told him to join the gang of workers who packed tins as they came off the machines. One of the gang, who had worked in the factory for over twenty years, had died of a stroke during the night. You're lucky, his brother said. Don't let me down.

No one bothered to show him how to tie up the tins and pack them into the cardboard cartons. He watched the others take six tins at a time off the conveyor belt, and in swift expert movements whip a piece of string round the bellies of the tins, flip them over, cross the string round them, and then toss the firmly-tied tins to someone else who dropped them into an open carton. It looked easy.

He moved to the edge of the conveyor belt, hesitated for a moment, then leant forward to pick up six tins. The tins tipped over and rolled on to the concrete floor with a loud series of clangs. No one seemed to be taking any notice of him. He stooped down and put the tins together on the floor. He pulled a piece of string out of the pile near the conveyor belt, wound it round the group of tins, and tried to flip them over. They slipped out of the noose and scattered across the floor. Someone laughed. He pretended he hadn't heard. He tried again. Same result. The third time he tried everyone was laughing and gathered in a circle around him. He looked up embarrassed and upset. One man imitated the clumsy way he had tried to tie the tins. This made the others laugh more. He didn't know what to do. He sprang up, ready to hit the nearest mocking face. Someone grabbed his arm from behind. He wheeled quickly and found himself staring into a pair of spectacles through which, because of their power, he could hardly see the eyes of the man who wore them. He stepped back. Everyone had stopped laughing.

The man in spectacles was very fat; he looked like an over-grown baby. He turned and shooed the others back to work. (They all seemed afraid of the man.) Kneeling down on the floor, the man gathered the tins, got a piece of string, and motioned to him to come closer. The man's hands moved quickly; the tins were tied. The man tossed the tins to him and pointed to a carton. He fitted them into the carton, feeling stupid for having got angry.

The man got more tins off the conveyor belt and, using emphasised gestures and sign language, started teaching him. By lunch time, he could tie the tins properly.

When he was alone with his wife that night he told her that he had befriended a papalagi.

He didn't see the man the next morning. During morning-tea time he mentioned the man to his brother and a group of Samoans he was with. They looked at one another. Then his brother told him that the man was *funny* and his wife was a *bad* woman. He expected them to explain further but they didn't. In the afternoon the man came again. He sensed everyone watching them, and he wanted to tell the man to go away.

The man came every afternoon for four days.

Every lunch hour he saw the man eating alone in the cafeteria. On Friday a small thin woman sat at the man's table. He observed them. They never talked. She seemed too preoccupied watching the men at the neighbouring tables.

Three months later he was told to shift to the next wing of the factory. Remembering that the fat man operated the main machine there, he told his brother he didn't want to shift. His brother said there was nothing he could do about it. However, as he worked with the man, their friendship grew. They gradually learnt to communicate adequately by means of a vocabulary of gestures and facial expressions and broken English. They laughed a lot and lunched together in the cafeteria. The man's wife never joined them. When his brother warned him again about the man and his wife he said the man was his friend. He noticed that the other Samoans in the factory were avoiding him. It didn't worry him.

One day the man asked him if he wanted to learn how to operate the machine. Frightened of the machine, he shook his head. The man laughed and slapped the control panel playfully. Like a baby, the man signalled, rocking his arms like a cradle. Next day the man showed him a simple diagram of the machine which baffled him. In sign language the man read the diagram for him. Then, pointing out each part of the machine on the diagram and using the machine itself, the man showed him how the parts worked.

Within two months he could operate the machine with the man's help. Near the end of the year, whenever the foreman wasn't around, the man let him operate the machine on his own.

Just before Christmas the factory held a picnic at a beach forty miles from the city.

He sat with his brother and their wives in the shade of some pine trees, watching their children playing on the swings and slides. It was hot but a cool breeze was starting to blow in from the sea over the sand dunes. A noisy rugby match between two factory teams was being played on the field in the centre of the camping ground. Near one sideline stood a row of beer kegs perched on wooden stands. Round them was a large crowd drinking and cheering. His brother went and joined them.

His youngest son slipped off the swing and started crying. He comforted him, put him back on the swing, and then wandered down to the rugby game. Many of the spectators were drunk already; they ran up and down the sidelines cheering loudly. He observed them disapprovingly. (He didn't drink; never had.)

A young player was dragged off the field with blood on his forehead. Some spectators poured beer all over him. The youth sprang up and chased them around the kegs, then he lay under one of the kegs and opened his mouth wide, and someone turned on the faucet. Everyone cheered as the beer streamed down into the youth's mouth. He saw his brother by the keg and went towards him, but his brother waved him away; his brother's friends laughed. A woman rushed forward and thrust a cold frothing glass of beer into his hand. Loud clapping erupted. He recognised the woman when she turned her back on him. It was his friend's wife. She looked like a skeleton in her flimsy bikini. She squealed with laughter as she hurled herself into the arms of a group of men. He turned and went towards the dunes, pouring the beer out of the glass as he went.

It was low tide; a lone seagull screeched as it hovered above the water a short distance from the beach; there was no one about; small waves pancaked on to the sand; the beach curved away and disappeared into the haze miles to his right. He inhaled deeply. The pungent smell of sea and sand and sky and decaying seaweed made him dizzy for a moment. He went down to the water's edge.

As he strolled along, the small waves washed round his feet and sucked the sand from under them. He stopped, picked up an interesting piece of driftwood, ran his fingers along it, snapped it in half, and threw the pieces into the waves. He thought of home.

He sensed that someone was watching him. He looked up at the dunes. The figure was unreal in the haze of heat swimming up from the sand. He shielded his eyes with his hands, and the figure came into sharper focus. His friend. He waved. His friend started down towards him. He looked ridiculous in his grey woollen suit and black shoes, and as ne waddled through the pulpy sand his spectacles glinted in the light.

They picked up flat stones and shells and skimmed them across the water as they walked. The man's shoes were soon filled with sand; they stopped and he shook the sand out of them. After eating some chocolate which his friend had taken out of his pocket, his friend said he was tired. He took him to have lunch with his family.

After lunch, during which his friend made everyone laugh by performing tricks with his handkerchief, the women took the children for a swim, and his friend left to look for his wife.

He tried to sleep in the shade but couldn't, so he sat up and watched the crowd beside the sports field. The kegs were now under nearby trees. Most of the people were still drinking heavily and cheering two youths who were wrestling near the kegs. Suddenly one of the youths jumped up and kicked his opponent viciously in the chest. They were soon pummelling each other with their fists. Some of the women poked fingers into their buttocks, encouraging them to fight on. One of the youths collapsed to his knees, blood streaming from his nose. A woman embraced him mockingly and licked the blood off his face. Another woman wrestled the other youth to the ground, rolled on top of him and, moving her hips up and down, kissed him. A man grabbed her from behind, lifted her up and, carrying her above his head, rushed through the cheering crowd and up over the dunes, with three other men chasing them. He remembered who the woman was, sprang up, and went after them. He tried not to run.

He scrambled along the tops of the dunes, keeping them in view as they ran along the water's edge. Just as they were disappearing round the next dune he stumbled and was winded by the fall. He struggled to his feet, fell down again, and tried sucking air into his lungs. They ran out of his hearing.

Minutes later he was peering over the dune's edge.

She lay naked on the sand, half-covered by the body of the man who had been carrying her, legs upraised and quivering like the wings of a crippled bird as the man pounded at her. One of the other men tried to wrench him away from her, but he kicked him away. The woman moaned. The man gasped and then rolled off her.

The other men took turns.

He rolled on to his back and exposed his eyes to the sun's punishing glare as though he wanted the light to burn out what he had seen.

The woman screamed. He forced himself to look again. Two men were now working at her. He realised she was enjoying it all. His loins tightened and he was aware that he had an erection. He hated the woman then.

He sprang up. Turned to go. Gasped when he saw his friend standing in his path. Lowered his head, brushed past him, and ran back over the dunes.

He would never be able to forget the sandpapery feel of the man's suit sleeve on his bare arm. Or the tears on the man's face.

The man and his wife did not return to work again.

He was given control of the man's machine a year or so later.

14

It was the last church dance of the year. He knew his parents weren't going: his father was ill with a cold. He asked the girl to go. He wanted her to meet some Samoans before she met his parents. When he saw her he knew that she was unsuitably dressed for the dance. She wore a tight mini skirt, bead necklaces, and leather boots which nearly reached her knees. He didn't say anything to her though; she had to find out for herself. He wore a dark suit and tie.

He told the taxi driver to go to his house first. She waited in the taxi for him. When he returned he was wearing a fawn corduroy sports coat, navy blue shirt, and dark grey trousers. She asked him why he had changed. The suit was too hot, he lied to her.

There were many people and cars outside the church hall. She put an arm through his as they approached it. Pretending he wasn't thinking about it, he took his arm away. Most of the people greeted him in Samoan. They stopped and he talked with some of them. No one spoke English. As they talked he watched her. He sensed she was starting to feel uncomfortable.

The small lobby of the hall was crowded. He recognised some of the people and greeted them. Many of the others were strangers to him, recent immigrants who were too shy and self-conscious to go into the dance. He held her hand and steered her through the crowd. She was trembling; he pretended not to notice.

Two deacons sat at the table in the doorway selling tickets. He knew both of them. He took her up to the table.

Both men asked him in Samoan why he hadn't come to church for so long. Before he could reply one of them said in Samoan: 'The lady is beautiful.' He laughed with them without looking at her. They asked if the girl went to university. He nodded. They congratulated him on getting his degree and sold him two tickets. Just before they went into the hall, one of the deacons reminded him not to forget God and his church.

'What were they saying?' she asked as they went in.

'Nothing,' he said. 'Only that you are very beautiful.' She moved into his side. He edged away.

The dance-floor was packed. On the small stage at the far end of the hall was the band — five youths playing amplified guitars. Their dark suits and ties, long hair, and guitars glistened under the stage lights: they reminded him of a row of wet magpies he had once seen on a farm fence. Most of the men in the hall wore suits and ties. The women were conservatively dressed. Many of them wore the traditional long skirt and half-frock. Nearly everyone wore leis. He saw some empty seats near the stage. The music ended. The dancers vacated the dance-floor quickly, leaving its glittering bareness to confront him. He started across it; the girl followed.

Even though there was still much talking and laughter, he sensed that the people were watching them. Many of the elders would be condemning their long hair and manner of dress. Nearly all of them would be watching the girl. He didn't see any other papalagi.

She was shaking visibly when they sat down. Again he pretended not to notice. The band started playing. He asked her to dance. She glanced round the hall. He knew she didn't want to dance until the dance-floor was crowded. He eased her up gently after six or so couples were dancing.

Hidden from the spectators, she moved into him. She looked up at him. He looked over her head and kept away from her.

'Don't other pakeha people come here?' she asked.

'Sometimes,' he replied.

When they got back to their seats, his brother and some of their friends were there. His brother got up and asked her to sit in his chair. As soon as they sat down, his brother and his friends crowded round him, ignoring her. They talked in Samoan even though they knew how to speak English.

'Beautiful girl!' some of them joked with him.

'Lucky fellow!' said his brother laughingly. They continued joking about her. He didn't even introduce her to them.

The next dance began. Without asking her, his brother bowed, held her reluctant hand, and took her to dance. His friends had scrambled across the floor and were now dancing. He watched them. She looked conspicuous among the dark suits and black hair and brown skins. His brother was talking continuously to her. She would simply nod and try to smile. Now and then he saw her look pleadingly across at him.

Returning alone when the dance ended, she sat down beside him and he noticed that she was on the verge of tears. He reached over to hold her hand. She withdrew it quickly, bit her bottom lip, and gazed at the floor. His brother came back with some bottles of orange. She refused a drink. They talked in Samoan while she sat there. He remembered and introduced his brother to her. She just nodded her head.

'Come on, cheer up!' his brother said to her in English. She smiled feebly. 'Don't get mixed up with these Samoan fellows. They love themselves too much to act civilised towards women. Take this snob over here. He feels a helluva lot for you yet he won't show it in public. At least not as long as other Samoan males are around to accuse him of being soft-hearted.'

The band leader announced that the next dance was to be a Samoan siva, and the band immediately started to play. A huge woman — wife of one of the deacons — leapt on to the floor. She danced, arms outstretched, hands weaving like birds. Everyone clapped. Two other women joined her. His brother sprang up, took off his suit coat,

and said to the girl, 'Watch how beautiful this fellow is!'
He whooped as he danced on to the dance-floor.

He pushed his leg against hers as they watched. She
moved her leg away. A girl he knew danced over to them
and bowed to him. He rose reluctantly, took off his sports
coat, and danced. His mother had insisted on teaching him
and his brother the siva when they were young. Yet he felt
embarrassed every time he had to perform it.

Dancing back to the girl, he bowed to her. She refused
to get up. He bowed again. She got up without looking at
him. He indicated to her that he wanted her to imitate the
way he was dancing. She tried. Some of the people
watching her laughed. He laughed too as he moved back
into the midst of the dancers. She followed him.

'Can we go now?' she asked as they walked back to their
chairs. He went and got his coat and they left.

He didn't say anything as they walked away from the
hall. He waited for her to start.

'Did you have to humiliate me that way?' she asked.

'How did I humiliate you?' he replied. He yearned to
comfort her but he had to know if she had learnt.

'How could you!' she said. 'Why did you have to make
me dance that ... that ... ?'

'Siva?' he said.

She pushed his arm away when he tried to put it round
her. 'They laughed at me!'

'I thought you'd enjoy it.'

'Enjoy it? I've never felt so humiliated before. And —
and why did they have to watch me all the time?'

'They weren't watching you.'

'But they were. I could feel it.'

'Now you know something of what it's like being part
of a minority group,' he said.

They caught a taxi and went to the coffee bar they
usually visited about once a week. They said nothing to
each other all the way there.

'If you sensed how I was feeling, why didn't you help
me?' she asked. He drank his coffee. 'Why didn't you?'

'I wanted you to find out for yourself. I could have helped you but I didn't want to.'

'Shit! You didn't want to?'

'No. I could've warned you, but I wanted you to find out for yourself.'

She bowed her head over her cup of coffee. In the dim light she looked as if she was crying softly. 'They despise us, don't they?' she asked, without looking up.

'Us?' he asked.

'I mean they despise us pakehas, don't they?'

He reached over and covered her hand with his. 'No,' he whispered. 'Some do but I think they have good reasons for doing so.'

Gazing into his face, she said, 'And you?' He looked away. 'I was never so frightened before. They all looked the same to me — a wall of staring faces stripping me like an insect put under a bloody microscope. Couldn't you have warned me just a little?'

'No one warned me,' he said. They remained silent. They were in a small cubicle away from the rest of the people, and the gloom shielded them from each other's scrutiny.

She reached across and gripped his hand firmly. 'Did you have to treat me as if I didn't mean anything to you?'

'I'm sorry I did it now.'

'Don't be sorry,' she said. 'I learnt — I think. It's a pity we aren't like those lizards that can change colour to fit their surroundings.'

'A shame we aren't all purple.'

She laughed softly and said, 'By the way, who was that scrumptious girl who invited you to dance?'

'A beautiful girl I used to know.'

'Are you sure it's "used to know"?'

'Positively sure,' he said. She slid over the seat to him. He put an arm round her and caressed her face.

'Your brother's very handsome,' she said.

'He's all right. Only a less handsome version of his kid brother though.'

She bit his neck. 'He was dead right. You Samoan

bastards are helluva vain. By the way, is it true Samoan men beat their women?'

'Who told you that?'

'Mother,' she said jokingly.

'Yes, we beat our women mercilessly. Got to keep them in their proper place.'

'Are you going to beat me?'

'Right now?'

She unzipped his fly and caressed him, sighing, and nuzzling his neck. 'Why not?'

'What shall I use for a whip?' he said, gently caressing her breasts through her dress.

Clutching him tightly, she whispered, 'What about using this? It's gentle and understanding; it talks very fluently and it can overcome all racial barriers. Or any other barrier that needs overcoming.'

> *Whip me gently,*
> *Whip me cool,*
> *Whip me lovingly,*
> *Until I drool.*

15

He hardly recognised her when she got out of the car in front of the church. She wore a dark suit, no bangles or makeup, and her long hair was pinned up under a funny white hat. He teased her about it. She winked at him. Meet the dream of the New Zealand middle-class hausfrau, she whispered. His father came to them; his mother awaited them on the bottom steps of the church.

He introduced her to his father who took her to his mother and introduced her in broken English. The woman held the girl's elbow and steered her up the steps and into the church. He followed with his father.

They were a few minutes late; the service had started. He could feel the congregation watching them as they walked down the aisle. His mother always insisted on sitting three rows from the front, directly below the pulpit. She made the girl sit between her and her husband. He sat in the row behind them.

The pastor announced the next hymn. His mother opened the Samoan hymn-book and got the girl to hold one side of it. His mother was one of the most uninhibited singers in the church. He awaited the girl's reaction to her singing. She didn't react at all. As he watched her during the hymn, it dawned on him that she was a very accomplished actress: it was as if she had grown up in the church and had known his mother for a long time. She belonged. After the service he would have to warn her that his mother was also an accomplished actress.

Love one another, the pastor began his sermon. Without love we will destroy one another. The pastor then described the many different types of love. As he listened, he realised that the pastor he had admired as a boy was avoiding talking about physical love between a man and woman; he simply mentioned it and then condemned it as sinful outside marriage.

He grew bored with the sermon and withdrew into his thoughts. Some years before, religion had suddenly become meaningless to him. It wasn't a matter of disagreeing with church doctrines and beliefs: he was just bored with it. When he told his parents they accused him of being arrogantly vain. It was that atheist learning at university, his mother said. How could anyone get bored with God's church? He left the room and from then on refused to discuss religion. Yet he continued to feel guilty about hurting them and not attending church.

He didn't want to meet the pastor, so when the service ended he went out the side door and waited for the others by the car. His father arrived first and told him that the pastor had asked after him and inquired why he didn't come to have discussions with him any more. Why don't you go? his father asked. He didn't answer. His father said that their whole way of life was based on the church. Without God we are nothing, he ended.

The girl and his mother were talking easily as they approached the car. I like her, his father whispered to him.

As they drove home, the two women continued chattering and laughing. He found that he wasn't embarrassed any more by the way his mother spoke English.

His mother had spent nearly a whole week cleaning the house, every nook and cranny. Because he wasn't working she had got him to clip the hedges, mow the lawns, and weed the flower beds. On Friday she had remembered the footpath and he had to scrub it. He asked her what she was doing all this for. She told him that she didn't want the daughter of a rich and important businessman to think they were ignorant Islanders who didn't know how to live like New Zealanders. On Wednesday night she brought out the family Christmas tree, and put it up in the sitting room. His father bought a new string of coloured lights and wound it all over the artificial tree that was already burdened with cotton snow and tinsel. When his parents brought all his certificates, diplomas, and trophies out of storage and started hanging them on the sitting-room wall, he objected. Why? she asked. He insisted that it was embarrassing. You should be proud of your education, she replied and flatly refused to take them down.

They also hung up framed photographs of his relatives in Samoa, group photographs of the Ladies Church Guild and deacons, and two large portraits of their two sons. His mother admired the gallery for a while, remembered something, went into her bedroom, and brought out a large Technicolor photograph of Mount Egmont which her husband had won at a sideshow. She crucified it to the centre of the main wall, admired it for a lengthy sighing time, and told him it was really artistic. He tried not to laugh as he left the room. He came into the sitting room the next morning to find four vases full of plastic flowers lined across the top of the mantelpiece. He replaced the plastic flowers with fresh flowers from the garden. She put the plastic flowers back that evening without saying anything to him. On Sunday morning before going to church to meet the girl, he sneaked fresh flowers into the vases. She put the plastic flowers back after he had gone, and locked the sitting room so no one could get into it until she had brought the girl home after the service.

When she was planning the menu for Sunday dinner, she asked him if he knew what the girl would want to eat. He said she would probably like to taste some Samoan food. She's not used to it and may get sick, his mother said. From previous experience he knew that she was ashamed to offer Samoan food to papalagi guests. To her, all papalagi ate bacon and eggs and toast and coffee for breakfast, roast beef or mutton and potatoes for lunch, and mincemeat or tinned spaghetti for the evening meal; for morning tea they had gingernut biscuits and hot cups of tea; for afternoon tea small cakes and hot cups of tea. And papalagi ate from expensive crockery and with polished knives and forks. Once he told her that papalagi used serviettes as well. She asked him what they were, and serviettes appeared the next time they had papalagi guests. His brother told her that papalagi always had a few drinks before their main meal and wine during the meal. What kind of drinks? she asked. Liquor, he said. At that point she delivered a short sermon on the evils of alcoholic beverages and threatened to disown them if they ever brought any into her God-fearing home.

So when the girl came for Sunday dinner they had orange drinks before the meal. After showing her the Christmas tree ablaze with lights, his mother took her to the wall (referred to by his brother as the 'Wailing Wall') and showed her all the certificates, diplomas, trophies, and photographs one by one. The photograph of Mount Egmont got special attention.

For the main course they had roast lamb, green peas, boiled cabbage and carrots, boiled potatoes, roast pumpkin, and thick brown gravy. Every time the food on the girl's plate diminished visibly, his mother heaped more on to it. For dessert they had pavlova, ice cream, and sliced chinese gooseberries. After that they had large slices of sponge cake and cups of tea. Then, while the men talked in the sitting room, his mother took the girl and showed her the whole house and her garden of potatoes and carrots in the backyard. Throughout all that time he worried about the girl's reaction to his home and family, especially to his mother. When his mother brought her back, he insisted he was going to wash the dishes. His mother protested, saying it wasn't a man's work to wash dishes. He gently but firmly pushed her into a chair and steered the girl into the kitchen and closed the door behind them.

She embraced him and said, 'I'm really happy.'

'You're not disappointed about not getting even a morsel of Samoan food?'

'No. Perhaps another day. I ate a helluva lot.'

'My mother wants to show you that she can be more

New Zealand than the New Zealander. Don't you think she imitates the papalagi middle class very well?'

'She's a wonderful person,' she said. She went over to the sink and turned on the hot tap. 'It's good to be in a real home.' He moved over and put his arms round her.

'It can be stifling,' he said. 'And there's little privacy.'

'In my home we have endless privacy. We want to be left alone to our terrible thoughts and fears.' She put the dishes into the sink. 'May I stay the whole afternoon?'

'Yes. And tonight if you like.'

'Won't your mother mind?'

'Not as long as we sleep in separate rooms and separate beds.' He caressed her thighs. She pushed him away playfully.

When they had finished washing and drying the dishes, she said: 'Do you think your parents like me?'

He hesitated. 'My father does,' he said.

'And your mother?'

'I don't know yet.'

'She prefers you to take out a Samoan girl, doesn't she?' He nodded. 'What if I got a handsome doctor to change the unreasonable pigmentation of my skin?'

'To what shade of the rainbow?'

'Green?'

'I'd unskin you,' he whispered. They laughed.

When they returned to the sitting room, his brother talked them into going for a swim. She didn't have a swim suit. His mother took her into her bedroom and gave her a floral lavalava and showed her how to tie it under her arms so that it covered her down to the tops of her knees. The men whistled at her when she returned. She pirouetted and bowed. He wanted to go to a more secluded beach but his brother insisted on going to Oriental Bay in the centre of the city. The girl did too.

There were few people in the streets; the city was left to the sun and to old people, sitting like plaster statues on bus-stop benches. The road curved along the shore a few feet above the beach. To their right, rows of houses, white like broken crockery, tiered the hillsides. The beach, about a hundred yards long, was crowded. Only a few unoccupied patches of sand were left. The city had emptied its winter-pale citizens to the precarious edge of the harbour.

They found a vacant parking space and parked the car. The girl and his brother got out quickly and raced for the steps leading down to the beach. He watched them from the sea wall as they ran through the crowd, dived into the water, and swam for the raft moored about eighty yards out. He had only been to Oriental Bay once before on a Sunday; his brother had argued him into going then. When they had got there he had refused to budge from the sea wall and his brother had gone for a swim on his own.

He got a lavalava out of the car and wound it round his waist to cover his tight swimming trunks and most of his legs. Some children stopped and stared at him. He winked at them. They giggled. He whipped off his lavalava. The children scattered. He laughed, put the lavalava on again, and headed for the steps.

Two middle-aged women wearing bikinis were coming up the steps. They stopped and looked up at him. He waited to let them pass. They continued up towards him, swaying their bulky hips more noticeably. He deliberately looked them up and down and concluded, with mounting amusement, that they had both shaved off their pubic hair. As the nearest one passed him, he patted her on the hip. She giggled and jumped one step up. Without looking at them, he went down the steps, knowing they were watching him. When he reached the bottom he stripped off his lavalava and waved it to them. They laughed.

Once on the sand he stretched and gazed up into the sun. Someone pounded on the sand. He looked down. A couple lying close together were staring angrily at him. His shadow covered them. The woman mumbled something to her man. He walked over to them. 'Why don't you do something?' he heard her say as he headed for the water.

At the water's edge he turned and surveyed the crowd. Whenever it was a hot summer's day, most papalagi exposed their bodies to the sun's agony, using various lotions to acquire suntans quickly. To Samoans a fair skin

71

was beautiful, so they avoided the sun. He remembered his brother, drunk at a party, telling an admiring papalagi divorcee that he had a permanent suntan, and that permanent suntan was really permanent and all-over. Next morning he had asked his brother if the woman had found out whether his permanent suntan extended even to the tip of his most hidden organ. They had laughed about it.

He left his lavalava on the beach and swam out to the raft. He was shivering with cold as he climbed on to it to find the girl and his brother lying on their backs as if asleep.

'So you worked up enough courage to come out, eh?' his brother said.

'Never knew you were that shy,' she said. He lay down beside her.

'Not when we're alone,' he whispered. 'How's your permanent tan?' he called to his brother.

'Peeling,' his brother said.

'Peeling all over?'

'No, it's safe where it's vital!' said his brother.

'In our islands what would all the worshippers of fair skins think of this girl?' he asked his brother, putting his arm round her.

His brother sat up, looked her up and down, and, shaking his head, said: 'Too skinny!'

She stood up, whipped off her lavalava, and strutted round in her wet bra and panties. 'What do you think now?' she asked.

'Still too underfed!' said his brother. She rushed over and rolled him off the raft into the sea.

Once in the water he called, 'This native's going to that over-populated beach to fish for an artificially-tanned shark.' He started swimming for the beach as they stood on the raft laughing.

That night she slept in the spare room next to his parents' bedroom. He expected her to come to his room during the night. She didn't, and he asked her about it in the morning before she went home. She didn't want to hurt his mother, she said.

After she left he found his mother in the kitchen and asked what she thought of the girl.

'I like her,' she replied, without looking at him. 'But I don't think she's suitable for you.'

'Why not?'

'She won't fit into Samoa.'

'Why not?'

'She doesn't know our customs, our ways of doing things. And our people won't accept her.' She turned, and gazing into his face said: 'Our way of life, our people, may destroy her.'

He left the house before she could say anything else, and walked the crowded Christmas streets. That evening he rang the girl and told her he loved her and was miserably happy because of it. She reminded him that they were starting their trip round the North Island in two days' time. Remembering it was Christmas the next day, he went and bought presents for his family and the girl. He bought her a collection of essays by Camus.

16

Samoa, our beloved home, is about two thousand miles from this cold country, their mother explained. (It was the middle of their third winter in New Zealand, and they were gathered in the sitting room near the electric heater, having just finished their evening prayers. They all wore thick pullovers and woollen slippers; the boys had blankets wrapped round them. Their mother's talk about Samoa and New Zealand was given often now, especially during the winter months.) In Samoa the sun shines nearly all the time, she said. It never gets cold. She warned her sons never to get caught in New Zealand rain. You can die of pneumonia, she said. (As she talked, the man fell asleep in his armchair, but the boys, who didn't know much about New Zealand yet, and even less about Samoa, remained attentively awake.)

In Samoa, she continued, the villages are clean and tidy and widely scattered round the coast — one has a lot of room to live in. New Zealand is crowded, noisy, and unhealthy. Families are crowded together but they don't care what happens through the walls, rooms, and hedges which separate them. (She had never left the confines of the city.) Samoa is lush green with tropical forests. New Zealand is made up of over-crowded cities rife with crime, especially murder. Samoans in Samoa never commit murder deliberately. Never trust papalagi strangers, she cautioned, they may be murderers or perverts, even the women. By the way, she added, most papalagi wear false teeth — papalagi food is too soft and full of dangerous chemicals. Papalagi are also physically weak; they age quickly from lack of hard manual work. Though she did not know any papalagi children, she declared that all papalagi children were rude, destructive, spoilt, and had no respect for their parents and elders. In Samoa, the children were the exact opposite, and she wanted them to be like all the other Samoan children.

The next time she talked to them, she began by saying that every Samoan in Samoa was a good Christian. Their whole way of life was centred round the Church which everyone respected and gave generously to. God gave us Christianity and only He can take it away; so our way of life can never die without Jehovah's consent, she reasoned. The papalagi brought Christianity to Samoa but then, as they gained in atheistic knowledge and worldly wealth and power, they forgot God and became pagans again. We have remained faithful to Jehovah's laws, she said; that is why Samoa is one of His Kingdoms on earth. Even here our Church is the fastest growing one. This is proof that we love God and He loves us. The few misguided Samoans who have forsaken the Church are paying for it: they lead sinful lives, drink and brawl in pubs, assault the police, and end up in gaol where they rightfully belong. These are the people who are giving us a bad name. What papalagi don't know is that these people are not *real* Samoans — they're half-castes. Remember always that a true Samoan is a full-blooded Samoan, and always be proud of your race and the Church which has given us so much.

There are no orphans or poor people in Samoa, she said another evening. No one starves either. We care for one another, sharing our material possessions equally. In papalagi countries there are hundreds of orphans, hundreds of poor people starving in the streets, and hundreds of old people dying in old people's homes. It is our duty to care for our parents and elders until they pass away. After all, they spent their lives caring for us.

Every time she talked of Samoa she ended by describing their family and village in vivid detail. When she discussed their family it was as if she was talking of bold knights of a bygone age of valour, justice, mercy, and bravery. She also described the other main families. She gave the role of villain to any family that had committed an injustice against their family. Conversely a good family she described as a valiant ally.

We Samoans, she concluded one night, must stand together, with God as our guide. If we don't, we shall be destroyed as the papalagi have destroyed the Maoris and Hawaiians.

And so she continued throughout the years, until a new mythology, woven out of her romantic memories, her legends, her illusions, and her prejudices, was born in her sons: a new, fabulous Samoa to be attained by her sons when they returned home after surviving the winters of a pagan country.

Her husband also contributed to the creation of this Samoa.

Pain is to be endured: this is the basis of Samoan manhood, he told his sons. A male is a man as soon as he can walk, and he must be able to suffer extremes of pain without a whimper. Fear is common to all men but a man must not be afraid of other men or allow himself to be insulted or mistreated. Without self-respect, life would have little meaning. A man's worth is measured in terms of courage; if he is a coward he might as well not live. In papalagi countries, he claimed, a Samoan man has personally to right the wrongs committed against him, especially when right and might — the scales of the law — are heavily weighted in favour of the papalagi majority. Christ taught us to turn the other cheek, but if one turns one's cheek and is slapped repeatedly then one should retaliate with a heavier blow and teach the tormentor that he is wrong. Whether one lives or dies after such an encounter does not concern the brave.

He taught his sons boxing, took them regularly to the major fights in the town hall, and exhorted them to model their behaviour on the Samoan professional champions of the New Zealand boxing circuit. The boys proved talented pupils — the younger became middle-weight champion at high school.

The role of a woman is to love her man, he explained one day. She must obey him in all things, give him children, and keep the home in order. A man's love for his wife and children must not be shown in public. Showing such affection publicly is a weakness peculiar only to women and papalagi. Love is a private feeling, something to be treasured and not revealed to the prying eyes of strangers. A good man must protect his family, provide for them the best way he knows how, and not betray their trust. Infidelity is a sin against God and against your whole family — the most sacred of institutions, and one upon which the whole Samoan way of life is based. Honour all your obligations to your family, church, and village, he said. Without your family you are lost, a bird without a nest to give you identity. You must sacrifice your personal ambitions if they clash with the wishes of your family. This is how it was in Samoa, how it is today, and how it will always be. God meant it to be that way.

Our culture is older than any papalagi culture, he declared one evening. Don't believe any papalagi who says otherwise. Our culture is also based on sacred laws sanctioned by God and handed down to us by our forefathers. That is why in Samoa we have been able to remain Samoan, safe from the changes brought about by rapacious papalagi.

The younger son treasured most of all his father's descriptions of the landscape. In Samoa, his father would say, the magnificent tropical forest is never far away. You can see it always, hanging at vision's end, watching you with the ominously loud silence of lava and black river boulder. And you are aware constantly of your own impermanence. Or the sound of children, like a mountain stream swirling over pebbles and boulders as smooth as the skins of your eyes, is always part of your day; and with so much youth around you, you are reminded of your own mortality and the need to live to the fullest every day of

77

your life. Or in Samoa it is difficult to accept death — everything invites you to live.

Years later the youngest son would admit to himself that almost all he knew of Samoa was a creation of his parents and other Samoans he admired. The only real memory he had was of the pig: he perfected that memory until every detail was fixed and final, more real to him than the Samoa his parents wanted him to inherit.

The boy sat on the high rock fence, munching a hunk of coconut. Below him the herd of swine squealed as they fought for the food scraps being tossed down to them by one of the boy's uncles. The stronger pigs bit and butted the smaller ones away from the food. Flies swirled round them and the air was dizzy with the stench of mud, pig excrement, and decaying food. The pigs grew quiet as their hunger was satisfied. The boy clapped his hands and threw the remainder of his coconut at the nearest sow.

His uncle and two other men went down to the pigs and walked among them. One of them suddenly gripped the hind legs of one of the largest pigs and pulled it out of the herd. It screamed and struggled. The other pigs scattered and were soon hidden in the undergrowth. The other men grabbed the pig's front legs and carried it up and over the rock fence.

The boy ran after them and joined the other children outside the kitchen fale. The men bound the pig's legs together with strips of bark. The boy noticed the pig's colour for the first time. It was black, and caked with thick patches of dried mud. After tying it up, the men went into the kitchen fale where a large umu was spitting flames. The pig struggled to break its bonds; it failed. It kept on screaming. The other children moved towards it. The boy followed warily.

He began to notice the animal's individual features. Two tusks curled out of the side of its mouth, their sharp tips were starting to pierce the hide immediately below its nostrils. Saliva and mucus dripped out of its mouth. He felt afraid — something terrible was going to happen; it had something to do with the helpless pig. Another child picked up a stick and jabbed it at the pig's belly. The pig screamed more loudly. The boy moved away from it.

One of the men came out of the kitchen fale with a long thick yoke and squatted down beside the pig. Two of the older children ran to him to take the yoke. The man called to the boy to come over. He went reluctantly. The man told him to go to the other side of the pig. It's your pig, the man said, extending the pole to him across the pig's throat. He refused to touch the end of the yoke. Take it, the man said. His hands closed round the end of the yoke. Now press down, the man instructed him. He looked away from the pig and pressed down. Harder, the man said. The pig screamed. This time it was more desperately high-pitched. Sit on the yoke, the man said. He sat down on the yoke as if he was sitting on the end of a seesaw. Good, the man said, smiling.

The pig heaved as the yoke began to sink down across its throat. Closing his eyes, the boy rocked up and down on the seesawing yoke. As the rocking rhythm continued, he relaxed and opened his eyes. One of his older cousins was now sitting on the opposite end of the yoke. The pig's struggling and screaming died down slowly; its tongue, coated with thick white froth, protruded from its mouth, beneath the magnificent tusks. His cousin started to laugh; he laughed too and put more effort into the rhythm. Up and down. Up and down. He felt as if he was floating. Free and floating. He placed his right foot on the pig's lower jaw; his left foot he rested on its chest and rocked harder, the end of the yoke he was sitting on thudding into the hard ground underneath him.

The pig's front legs died first; the hind legs twitched and stabbed into the choking air for a while longer, and then stopped abruptly.

His uncle came, examined the pig, and told them it was dead. The boy got off the yoke. His uncle patted him on the head and said that the pig would taste delicious when they ate it that night. The boy remembered that he was leaving with his parents for another country the next day.

He looked down at the dead pig. Flies were trailing into its mouth and nostrils. He caught his reflection in the pig's left eye. He cried as he ran to his mother in the main fale.

That night, at the farewell feast, he refused to taste the pork. It was as if he had not wanted to taste his own flesh, he would think years later.

17

His mother came into his room while he was packing his suitcase and told him she didn't want him to go on the trip. He continued packing as if he hadn't heard her. You don't know what might happen out there, she argued. Convinced by his silence that she couldn't change his mind, she helped him to pack. After a while he noticed that she was crying but he didn't say anything. She eventually asked if he was going with the girl. He nodded. Just before leaving the room she said it was a sin to be with a woman outside of marriage. He maintained his silence. She left the room.

He lay down on his bed and gazed at the ceiling. She returned and tossed a small bundle of pound notes on to his stomach. You will need some money, she said. She went out again before he could thank her.

Early the next morning his father and brother gave him some more money, told him to have a good time exploring 'Mamma's pagan land', and went off to work. He had breakfast with his mother. They didn't speak.

They heard a car pull up in front of the house. He went out and brought the girl into the kitchen. Immediately his mother acted as if she wasn't upset about anything. She insisted on the girl having something to eat, and as the girl ate she talked happily about their trip. The girl got out a road map and showed her all the routes they were going to follow and all the places they would visit. When they got up to leave, his mother kissed the girl and told her to ring or send a telegram if anything went wrong.

His mother accompanied them to the road. Just before he got into the van he saw tears in her eyes. He embraced her briefly and got in beside the girl. Be careful, she called in Samoan. Come back safely. She didn't wave as the van drove away, as though she was too frightened to.

The traffic was heavy on the main highway out of the city but they soon reached the outer suburbs where the houses and shopping centres all looked alike and there were few trees. It was getting hot; he unbuttoned his shirt and lowered the window.

The girl explained that the van would be their home for the following weeks; it carried everything they needed, even a rifle. Very efficient, he said. Ever since she was ten, she said, her father had taken her camping every Christmas vacation; he had taught her how to fish, swim, even hunt for deer. Was he good with a rifle, she asked. He shook his head.

Towards noon they were driving uphill alongside a deep gorge, following a river. Both sides of the gorge were densely forested. They rounded a bend. The girl slowed down and then stopped on the edge of the road overlooking the deepest part of the gorge. They got out, went over to the barbed wire fence, and gazed down at the river. The side of the gorge dropped away sharply from under them, and only a few ferns and creepers clung to it. Below, the river meandered through virgin bush. She told him she had often camped with her parents at the bottom of the gorge by the river. She suggested they should have a swim and lunch. She drove the van off the road into the shade of a high stand of trees and cut some sandwiches.

As they made their way down through the trees over the precariously steep track, he asked her to tell him the names of the trees and ferns. Rimu, tawa, ponga were some of the names she knew. He hadn't heard silence for a long time; he was hearing it now and it unnerved him. Rocks, unlodged by their feet, rolled away down through the trees. He often stumbled over fallen tree trunks and protruding roots. She laughed and helped him up. Soon his clothes were drenched with the smell of dank earth and rotting leaves and tree sap. She moved a few paces ahead of him. As he watched how sure she was in the bush, which was completely strange to him, he felt a deeper need to know her and through her his country of exile. The roar of the river grew louder, and the bush was suddenly alive with butterflies, moths, and gnats.

As soon as they broke from the trees on to a narrow expanse of stones and pebbles, she stripped off all her clothes, undid her hair, ran to the left to where the river was still and blue and deep, and dived in. She came up laughing, her long hair plastered to her face, neck, and shoulders. Come on, she called. But they can see us from the road, he said. Who cares, she said laughingly, and turned on to her back and floated. He undressed slowly, embarrassed. Everything off, she called. He left his underpants on and waded into the water. The sand felt slippery under his feet.

'It's bloody cold,' he said when the water was up to his armpits. She swam towards him, dived under, grabbed the sides of his underpants, and tried to pull them down. Crouching down in the water, he locked his arms round her shoulders and lifted her up to the surface.

She laughed and embraced him fiercely, rubbing her firm breasts against his chest, and twining her legs round his waist. 'Are you still cold?' she asked. He pushed her head down into the water and out again. He lifted her up. She squealed with laughter as he threw her away from him into the water. He scrambled out of the water and stood on the bank laughing at her. 'Come on,' she called. 'It's not fair you leaving your chastity belt on.'

'It's my first baptism in a Kiwi river and I don't want be caught with my pants down and my arse purple with cold!' he said.

She splashed him with water. 'Come on,' she coaxed. 'I promise if any religious campers come by I won't tell them you were trying to rape me. I'll just say you're my brother, but we happen to be different shades because mother had you during a thunderstorm.'

'Promise?'

'I promise.'

He turned his back and took off his underpants. She clapped and whistled. 'Close your dirty eyes or you'll go blind!' he called. He looked over his shoulder at her. She closed her eyes. Wheeling swiftly, he dived into the water and raced past her to the opposite bank where he lay half immersed in the water on a narrow sandbank.

'You dropped something,' she called.

'What?'

'I think we Christians call it innocence.'

She swam over and lay beside him on her back, her head resting on the sand above the water. He turned on to his side to face her and said, 'They can see us from up there.'

'Bugger them,' she replied. 'Anyway it's about time they looked at some beautiful people.'

'You know something?'

'What?' she said, without looking at him.

'This is the first time I've seen you naked and in broad daylight.'

'Am I okay?'

'Need a few improvements here and there.'

'Liar,' she said. She took his hand and rubbed it over her belly. Droplets of water glistened on her breasts. He bent down and licked them off. She pulled away from him and swam to the deepest part of the river, near the opposite bank. Treading water, she beckoned to him to come over to her.

Once she was in his arms, he pulled her back until they were both standing on the river bottom, heads above the slow-moving water.

'Have you ever made love to anyone in a river before?' she asked. He shook his head. He kissed her deeply, her mouth and eyes and ears. She purred softly in his arms. She told him that she had forgotten to take her pill the night before. He started to release her but she caressed him with her hands and made him strong and directed him into her warmth.

She stretched and flowed round him, the sun trapped in her eyes as she gazed up into the sky, her head flung back lazily into the water, her hair swirling round her face and shoulders. She was the river itself with all its rhythm and weaving and turning and pull.

'I love you, love you, love you,' she murmured.

She tensed round him, as if the river itself had stopped still, and uttered her coming into his mouth with teeth and tongue and gasping breath. He pulled out just before he came.

His sperm, a white string in the blue of the water, curled up to the surface between them. For a slow moment it brushed against her breasts; then, caught in the current, it flowed away from them.

'What a waste,' she sighed.

They decided to camp there for the night. After eating their sandwiches, she sunbathed naked. He brought down the tent and other supplies. Then he went to sleep in the shade of some nearby trees.

In the late afternoon she taught him how to put up the small tent. He cut supple branches and spread them out on the tent floor and covered them with blankets. They gathered some firewood. She showed him how to light a fire. She joked about how helpless he seemed outdoors. Didn't all Samoans use outdoor fires for cooking, she teased him. Those were Samoa-Samoans; he was a New Zealand-Samoan, made helpless by the comforts of electricity, instant food, and over-efficient women, he replied.

She woke up during the night and found him sitting outside the tent beside the dying fire. She wrapped a blanket round her and went and sat beside him. He explained that he couldn't sleep because of the beat of the river, the silence, and the strange sounds of the bush. He was afraid of it all. She coaxed him back into the tent and made love to him slowly, gently.

He fell asleep soon after, with the sound of the bush and river washing through his mind, healing it.

Rivers soothe the pebble's ache
and shape islands to come.

18

The narrow plain of neat paddocks, crisscrossed by orderly
barbed wire fences and hawthorn hedges, stretched ahead
between two low ranges as far as they could see. She asked
him to stop the van. He was glad to. He had been driving
for almost three hours and his back and eyes were aching.
He parked under some trees on the roadside. Nothing
moved on the plain. In the bright sunlight it glowed like
a meticulously painted landscape on a tourist poster. About
a mile ahead a dirt road branched off to the left and
nudged its placid way across the plain between two rows
of pines to a spacious white farmhouse with wide verandas.
Behind the house stood a group of sheds surrounded by
wooden stockyards. He took a bottle of beer out of a carton
he had bought in the last town they had passed through,
opened it with his teeth, and offered it to her. She didn't
want it, so he sipped it leisurely, waiting for her to explain
why she had wanted to stop there. He lay back in the seat
and closed his eyes.

'We used to own that once,' she said.

'All that prettiness out there?' he asked.

'A part of it,' she said. 'I have a history too, though it's
not as old as yours or the Maoris' who owned the plain
before we robbed them of it. I'm not very proud of it, but
it's enough to prove I have roots in God's Own Country.'
She took off her sunglasses and, gazing at him, told him
how her family had acquired part of the plain.

Once upon a time, she began, the plain and the
neighbouring hills and valleys were ruled by a Maori tribe.

A series of prosperous pas dotted the plain and the range to the east. Because the area was so remote it was one of the last to feel the full impact of the pakeha.

But the pakehas came all right: first the missionaries selling the new God for converts, and then the traders selling muskets for flax. For a start, the tribe tolerated the missionaries, but only a few souls — usually those of slaves — were saved. Only a few muskets were sold at first too: usually to chiefs who bought them as status symbols. But after neighbouring tribes using muskets began to raid the area, the traders flourished richly. To get money to buy muskets, the people shifted to the swamps to cut flax. Soon many of them began to die from influenza, pneumonia, mumps, and venereal disease — all pakeha-introduced. Dizzy with dreams of conquest and of settling old scores, the warriors fought bigger and more frequent campaigns. The tribe began to die. Finally, to save themselves, the people turned to the missionaries and their promises of peace and salvation, and, backed by the Crown, the missionaries established some semblance of law and order in the area.

Then came crowds of settlers who bought much of the land with cheap goods and lies. But the tribe was still too strong for the settlers to move in and claim their largely dishonest purchases. And as the tribe saw land in other parts of the island being lost, they joined some other North Island tribes under an elected king. These King Maoris wanted to live in peace with the pakeha but they would not sell any more of their land.

But we found an excuse for war. The Maoris, we argued, are stone-age savages who are hindering progress, and they're secretly conspiring to wipe us out. So for about a decade, off and on, we fought them — with the help of British soldiers. After we'd defeated them in a very un-British-gentlemanly sort of way, we made them pay for our wars by confiscating thousands of acres of their land. Compensation, we called it. We even took large areas from the tribes who'd helped us in the wars!

And so my Protestant family arrived on the scene. My grandfather, an unemployed and visionary plumber from Manchester, and my grandmother, a frail servant girl, came to New Zealand in 1879. They met on board the good ship *Adam Tool* (or some name like that), and got married as soon as they set foot on the promised land. As well as their marriage vows they also vowed to make a fortune as quickly as possible and return to England, the constantly pregnant Mother Country.

He befriended a land agent who had acquired deeds to the confiscated plain through influential politicians. The agent was too scared to claim the plain himself, so he got my grandfather to lead an expedition of armed constabulary and push the remnants of the tribe off the land. As payment grandfather received a third of the plain and all the bush, pigeons, rocks, streams, eels, sacred burial grounds, empty pas, and ghosts.

Being British (and a certified plumber) grandfather didn't believe in leaving the land as it was, or in tapu, ghosts, and eating rats. He believed fervently in Progress under the British Flag and God's Protection and in converting the bush into meadows populated by gambolling snow-white lambs and the English landed gentry riding stallions.

He tore down the central pa, and on the site put up a small shack made of axe-hewn logs and manuka branches cemented with mud. He brought his wife to the shack. When she saw it she said she wanted to go back to England at once. He promised to take her back as soon as the land had yielded him its magnificent riches. How long? she asked. A few years, he promised. The 'few years' were to extend to eternity for both of them.

With only a horse, two hands, two axes, a box of plumbing tools, and an abundant dream, he set out to conquer the bush. Within five arduous years, the shack was surrounded by a small farm with a few milking cows and sheep, and ferocious dogs to keep roving Maoris away from their burial ground (and from his wife, so grandfather later told his descendants).

My grandmother had two children in quick succession. They both died soon after they were born. My grandfather forgot to help make more heirs as he drove himself against the bush. He used fire, and for lengthy periods the plain choked with flame and smoke. Fire brought him quicker prosperity, which enabled him to hire farm workers and buy machinery, which in turn speeded up the clearing of the bush. Bare of its cover, the land on the hills eroded, and periodic floods threatened to destroy all that he'd built — a comfortable home, flocks of sheep, and a dairy herd. He levelled all the pas and used the rocks from them to dam the main stream and direct it on a new course well away from the house. One day he found one of his farm hands dead in the middle of one of the burial grounds. So he avoided the burial grounds and farmed only the land round them.

Twenty years later he was a dynamic force in local politics: chairman of the local farmers' association, a prominent member of the Anglican church, a large shareholder in many of the businesses in the nearby town, liked and respected by all the local farming community. He also owned the most beautiful house in the district; its plumbing was envied by everyone. Above all else he had two sons. He had sired them at the age of fifty when he didn't have to use all his energy fighting the bush, floods, erosion, livestock pests, and weeds. After his sons' birth he lost interest in his wife as a 'comfort'. The flesh, he would tell his heirs, was not to be trusted; trust only God and yourself; all good men are self-made.

They planned to visit England for his sixtieth birthday. A week before they were due to leave he had a heart attack. He was confined to a wheelchair for the rest of his cantankerous life. He died in 1938, a year before his sons went to the war.

After studying at university, his sons had refused to return to the farm. One became an accountant, the other a lawyer. He threatened to disown them, but he still helped to promote their careers. Just before he died, grandmother sent for his sons. He didn't recognise them; he was in too much pain and too much afraid. He didn't want to die despite his devout belief in the Afterlife. Just before exhaling his last breath, he mumbled something about the bloody bush and land having beaten him. For the first and only time they heard him use a four-letter word: Fuck the Maoris, he cursed. Fuck'em! Then he was dead.

The day after he was buried in the cemetery of the nearest town he'd helped to plant, his sons returned to their respective cities. They promised their mother a black marble tombstone with a cherub on it for their father; they also promised to visit her often. She refused to let them shift her into a town house. So they hired a manager for the farm, and a refined lady companion for her.

When the war began, the accountant son signed on eagerly. The lawyer tried various manoeuvres to evade conscription, but he failed.

The accountant joined the air force, qualified as a bomber pilot, and returned from the war with a few modest decorations. The lawyer got a safe post as defence lawyer in military court cases, but he didn't return — he died with his commanding officer's nubile mistress in a civilian motor accident. The traffic police, so the story went, found him with his hand still lodged between his companion's thighs.

The accountant returned to a grief-stricken mother, and found it easy to persuade her to sell the farm and go to live in a town house. She died four months later. Her son ordered a tombstone exactly like her husband's, paid off her companion, and sold the town house.

From the missionaries, the traders, the wars, and his pioneering parents, my father inherited a comfortable fortune, she ended. She sat gazing at the plain for a while. Then she asked him for a beer. He gave her a bottle, and drove on until he found a suitable spot to camp by a stream a short distance from the main road. He ripped open the carton of beer, and they talked and drank steadily.

'If you visit any Kiwi museum, you'll have to look bloody hard to find the ancient tikis the Maoris placed in front of their meeting houses,' she said. 'When you find a tiki — they're usually hidden away in a remote corner — you'll notice that its most stimulating organs have been chiselled off. The missionaries came with chisels as well as Bibles. My ancestors (and most of their illustrious descendants) were scared of the third hand, the one that can inject life to give birth to all mankind.'

That night they were both merrily drunk when they went to sleep on the mattresses in the back of the van.

> Show me the way to go home,
> I'm sozzled and I want to go to bed,
> I had a little drink about an hour ago
> And it's gone right to my head.
> Wherever I may roam,
> On land or sea or foam,
> You will always feel me
> Injecting this song,
> Show me the way to come home.

19

He woke before sunrise. His throat was parched and a dull ache throbbed in his head. He left the van without waking the girl, got a bucket, and went down to the stream.

All round him the bush was webbed with mist which shone like thin silk in the waking light. When he lay down on the bank of the stream, the dew numbed his hands and body. He thrust his head into the water; the cold shocked the ache out of it. Gasping loudly he jumped to his feet. His ears rang with pain. He stripped off his dirty shirt and dried himself with it. Some sheep, wet wool matted with dirt, stood on the opposite bank watching him. He scooped up a stone and threw it at them. The sheep retreated to a safe distance, stopped, and watched him again. He filled the bucket, pulled it up, and went back to the van.

The girl was still asleep. He quietly collected all the empty beer bottles and tossed them into the undergrowth. A dog barked down in the plain from the direction of the farm house hidden from view by the trees.

He made a small fire and put the billy on to boil. As he sat gazing into the flames, he realised he was no longer afraid of the bush and its ominous silence. It had somehow eased into him and made him part of it.

The billy would take a while to boil, so he got up and followed a faint track uphill through the trees and dense undergrowth. Leafy branches, ferns, and creepers whipped at him, drenching his trousers with dew. At first the cold dew stunned his bare arms and chest, but as he pushed his way through the foliage he gradually felt invigorated.

He broke through the stand of bush and found himself on the edge of a number of paddocks which spread up before him in a series of hills. The dew glittered in separate drops on the grass blades, making the whole area sparkle like a stretch of shimmering water.

He climbed to the summit of the hill immediately in front of him, sat down on a flat-topped boulder, and gazed down at the plain and across it to the eastern hills. The sun, now half over the hills, blinded him, and he looked down at the plain smoking with mist. The narrow column of smoke from the fire he had made rose out of the trees at the bottom of the hill.

As he gazed at the plain he remembered the girl's story. The light grew brighter and the farm house and sheds came into sharper view through the lifting mist. He let his thoughts wander until they floundered on the reefs of disturbing conclusions about himself. The more he struggled to avoid these reefs, the sharper and more painful they became.

The mist was disappearing quickly from the plain. The cloudless sky seemed to suck it up in long-drawn-out gulps. A man dressed in pyjamas came out on to the farm-house veranda. A dog pounded up to him. The man clutched it by the neck and flung it back down the steps. It landed on its back with a painful yelp and scurried off behind the house, tail between its legs. The man looked up at the sky for a moment and went back into the house.

To his left, in a shallow gully at the bottom of the hill, a line of sheep was snaking its slow way through sparse stands of flax and manuka. When the line reached the narrow top end of the gully it broke apart. Some of the sheep started up towards him. The others began making their docile way up the side of the adjacent hill.

Momentarily he was frightened by the unusual sound. It was like the beating of a huge heart. He surveyed the hills around him. Nothing. He listened again, and recognised the sound of slowly beating wings. He glanced up.

The hawk seemed to have been born out of the sky itself. It hovered above him, its outstretched wings pulsing in the still air, the sunlight caught in its talons. The sheep which were coming up the hill saw it and froze in their tracks; then the leader broke and ran back down the gully; the others followed. The hawk moved across the sky and hovered above the gully. Fascinated, he observed the bird, then the sheep — all now cowering in the gully among the flax and manuka, then the bird again. This was the first live hawk he had seen, and he was beginning to comprehend the beauty of fear, the awesome depth of freedom. Poised in the sky, the hawk seemed to be holding up the earth. The silence trembled as it dropped lower, stopped, hovered again. He remembered his father telling him that their family god in the 'days of darkness' (as he called the time before the missionaries came to Samoa) was the owl. His father had described how his father, the healer, had often taken him when he was a small boy into the centre of the palm groves, and in the evening had waited for an owl to fly through the gloom. Then he had whispered to him: 'He is still here. He has not forsaken us.' Once they had hidden in a clump of bushes and watched an owl swoop down from nearby trees, catch a rat in its talons, tear the rat's heart out with its beak, and devour it. Perhaps to the Maoris the hawk had been a god, he thought. Then he remembered that the hawk had come with the pakeha.

The rifle shot severed the silence which held the hawk and the hills together, and echoed across the sky. He scrambled to his feet. For a hopeful instant he thought the hawk would continue to balance the earth on its delicate axis, but it folded and plummeted, like a fist, down from the sky into the gully. The sheep scattered.

'Good shot, eh!' the girl called.

She was standing at the edge of the trees at the bottom of the hill. Dressed only in a lavalava, she looked completely incongruous against the backdrop of trees; the dew-green grass before her; the sky void of meaning; the heavy rifle cradled in her arms like a sleeping child. She waved to him and began to run up the hill.

A short distance up, she stumbled to her knees. The lavalava fell away from her. She picked it up, draped it round her neck, and laughed as she continued naked up the hill. Before she reached him he wheeled and started down the gully. He stopped himself from running.

The hawk lay spread-eagled across a flax bush. The shot had pierced a ragged hole through its breast and out through its back, shattering the spine. He clutched the feathers at the tip of one of its wings and marched back up the hill, dragging the hawk behind him on the ground.

He threw the hawk at her feet. 'Did you have to?' he asked.

She stepped towards him, stopped, said: 'It's only a hawk.'

In silence he continued staring at her. 'It was after those poor sheep. I *had* to kill it!' She wrapped the lavalava round her body and looked away from him.

Kneeling down beside the hawk, he started to rip out the large feathers at the wing-tips. He worked with a quiet fury. She knelt down to help him. He pushed her away. She stood watching him.

He finished plucking the feathers, dug a hole with his hands, stuffed the hawk into it, covered it with soil, and stamped the earth down with his feet.

'You don't have to be angry about it,' she said.

Grabbing two fistfuls of feathers, he started down the hill. 'Anyway what the hell are you going to do with those?' she called.

'Eat them!' he shouted back without turning round. 'Your lily-white ancestors ate everything else that was worth anything in this fucken area. Now you even want to kill the bloody scavengers you brought with you!' He immediately regretted what he had said. He wheeled to apologise to her.

She rushed down at him. He caught her and tried to stop her fists beating at his face, her knees jabbing at his groin. But she fought him off and came at him again. 'I'm sorry!' he shouted. He couldn't stop her so he slapped her hard across the face. She fell down and cried into the grass. The feathers he had been holding lay scattered round her. He picked up her lavalava and tried to wrap it round her. She slapped his hands away.

'I'm sorry I got angry,' he said. She kept on crying. He went up and got the rifle, which she had left at the top of the hill.

On his way down he stopped and looked at her. She refused to look up at him. He collected most of the feathers and went down to the van.

He fried some eggs and bacon and waited for her. He heard her make her way through the undergrowth and stop a few paces behind him. He put some food on to a plate and handed it to her. She took it and came and sat opposite him across the fire. They ate in silence.

'I'm sorry,' she said.

Then he explained to her why the killing of the hawk had angered him. 'Perhaps it was the only beautiful creature left in the plain,' he said. 'The only wild creature left. A scavenger but free like the owl my family used to worship in ancient times.'

'But there are other hawks here,' she said.

'It was my first hawk. I may never see the others. For me, all that's left in this area now is a domesticated farmer who hates dogs; domesticated sheep and cows — blood of the Kiwi welfare state; perhaps a very domesticated farmer's wife; lots and lots of domesticated grass . . . and the memory of a hawk.'

'I just didn't think,' she replied.

'We never do, do we?' Before she could reply he began to collect the dirty dishes. She sprang up and went into the van.

She had packed everything when he returned from the stream. She wore a pair of orange shorts and a blue sweater and she was sitting by the fire, stirring the dying embers with a stick. He put the bucket of dishes into the van and came and sat opposite her. The mist had vanished completely. Birds — he didn't know the names of any of them — cried from the high canopy of trees above them. He smelt the fecund odour of damp earth drying in the sun.

She glanced at him, saw him looking at her, and looked down at the fire again.

'Are you still angry?' she asked. When he didn't reply she looked at him. He smiled at her. She got up to come over to him but he said not to. He had many things to tell her, he said, conclusions about himself, which, while he was sitting on the hill, the plain and what she had told him about it had forced him to face.

He despised Maoris, he confessed. (Maybe despised was too strong a word.) Anyway he had always treated Maoris in a condescending manner. He was also suspicious of them. Like many other Samoans, he thought himself superior to Maoris. Because of this, he had never really tried to befriend any of the Maoris he had known at school, at the places he had worked at, and at university. He admitted that most Samoans believed the same racist myths about Maoris as pakehas did: Maoris were dirty, lazy, irresponsible; they were intellectually inferior; they lacked initiative, drive, courage; they drank too much, were sexually immoral, treated their children cruelly; all that most of them were good at was rugby, bulldozer-driving, dancing, and playing in bands; the only Maoris who had made the grade and were now teachers, doctors, lawyers, and politicians were the descendants of Maori royalty; the quicker the Maoris adjusted to the pakeha way of life, which was based on thrift and cleanliness and godliness, sobriety and honesty and hard work, the quicker they would become worthy New Zealand citizens. He paused for a moment and then said that it was funny how these were the very myths that pakehas believed about Samoans (and about Islanders in general).

Most Samoans also believed that Maoris lacked pride. They had given in too easily to the pakeha and were no longer true Polynesians. Most of them couldn't speak their own language and knew little of their ancient way of life. We are the only true Polynesians left, his father had said. Watch a Samoan walking down the main street of this city and you will see a man who has total pride in being

Samoan. Watch a Maori and you will see someone who is ashamed of being Maori, of being a man.

Do you know that the most vicious fights in the pubs and billiard saloons and at parties in the city are between Maoris and Samoans? he asked her. He had taken part in a few of them. A small group of Maoris came into a predominantly Samoan billiard saloon and started winning at a crowded pool-game. He helped his brother and some of their friends beat them up and chase them out into the street. In turn he was beaten up at a party where he had gone to bring his drunken brother home. Three Maoris worked him over. He spent four days at home in bed, bruised and bloody. Once, during the school vacation, he had played for the chief Samoan rugby team in the city. The opposing team was mainly Maori. A brawl erupted soon after the game started. A carload of policemen had to be called in to break it up. Many people had to be taken to hospital.

Go a stage further. We don't get on with Niueans, Tokelauans, or Cook Islanders. You would think, because Maoris and Islanders are at the bottom of the social and economic ladder here, we would be brothers. But the sad fact is we're not.

Last year at university an African student gave a lecture on racism in New Zealand. For over an hour he accused, condemned, and flagellated the pakeha; and I grew drunk with self-righteous anger, his anger. At question time a nervous pakeha housewife asked who had discriminated against him in the worst way. I awaited his answer eagerly, hungrily. 'PAKEHAS!' I expected him to spit out. You know what he said — sadly, almost as if he didn't want to betray his own colour, his own kind: 'ISLANDERS AND MAORIS!' Lies! I wanted to shout at him. Another Samoan student sprang up and took the word out of my mouth. The African, magnificent in his traditional robes — and I can see him now in all his truth — just smiled, looked down at him and said, *'You know the score, brother.'* Paused. Walked off the stage.

So you see, I suffer from a touch of racism. If I hadn't met you, hadn't come on this trip, I wouldn't have confronted that in myself; wouldn't have realised how absurd everything is.

He asked her if she had read any Polynesian mythology. She shook her head. He explained that the absurdity in life was at the core of all Polynesian myths and was especially evident in the saga of Maui, the legendary Maori hero. She asked him to tell her some of the tales. They would make her randy, he said. She said she would welcome that, and laughed.

Maui, he is sired by a god on a mortal woman, so he is half-god and half-man, he began. He is cast up out of the sea as a clot of blood. An old woman finds him and shapes him with love. Maui he grows up cheeky as morning, braver than all other he-men. (Don't forget, there are she-men.) One day, while he is working in his kumara patch, he finds the day is too short — the sun whizzes too fast across the heavens. So he weaves a magic net and he snares the sun in it. While he is beating the daylight out of Mr Sun, he says: 'Mr Sun, you go slow, man, or I come again and beat the dung out of you!' Mr Sun he agrees because he is a coward. So now you know why we associate cowardice with being 'yellow'. It is the colour of Mr Sun. And now you know why our day is twenty-four hours long.

Another time Maui he goes fishing with his brothers, who are jealous of him because he is their mother's favourite. Freud did not discover the Oedipus complex. On this fishing trip Maui fishes up out of the briny deep the large hunk of rock we now live on, kill one another on, and simply defecate on, to use good Kiwi English. That is why, if you read any of our tourist pamphlets, Kiwi-land is daintily referred to as 'The Fish of Maui!'

Before Maui took heavenly bodily form in our unworthy midst, we lived in darkness, secreting the inhuman in us that we still secrete today. There was no fire to commit arson with, to cook our brother with. Maui he climbs to heaven, and, while the gods are preoccupied with a delicious orgy of all kinds of healthy exercises now classed as sins by our puritan brethren, he steals some fire and brings it to earth.

So you see, Maui he is all He-man. He challenges all the gods and gets away with it. He is a better prole than Marx, a better warrior than Hitler, a better fornicator than Calvin, a better marcher than Mao, a more inventive masturbator than Hugh Hefner, a better visionary than Jesus — whose only achievement was turning the cross into a revered symbol, a better revolutionary than Che Guevara, and a hipster who makes Norman Mailer look like Liberace.

Maui, because of his human half, gets rashly brave and decides to challenge Hine-nui-te-Po, the death goddess. As an over-educated university genealogist, let me trace her bloodline:

In the beginning when the earth is bald, there is only Tane, father of man. After aeons of bachelor boredom, with only himself to play with, he decides to make himself a live mate (as you Kiwis would call such a creature). Extremely vain, he sits on the beach one day and out of sand he makes a figure after his own image. He breathes life into it. The figure it rises up. Tane he walks round it, admiring his handiwork.

He soon notices that his creation has no middle organ down where he, Tane, has an organ. Now it is understandable why Tane forgot that. After all he'd never before used his organ except to urinate with it. Gods, like us, tend to forget organs that are used only for ungodlike functions. His creation stares longingly at Tane's middle self. Tane looks down and sees his middle self all upstanding and conducting music with the sea breeze. He realises that his creation wants his organ for itself. Penis envy, we Freudians call it. And Tane, being a charitable god, decides to give his organ to his organless creation, but not permanently. After all Tane he has to piss now and then. Tane he is not sure where his creation wants him to put the organ. He stabs it at its knee. It shakes the head. He stabs it at its belly-button. It shakes the head. He stabs it at its left ear. It shakes the head. Tane he gives up, but his creation it grabs Tane's person — so a policeman would have reported to his superiors — and puts it between its legs.

'S-HE!' exclaims Tane, feeling all his loneliness disappearing fast. So his creation comes to be known as SHE, the first woman. And Tane and She fall to the sand and make thunderous music.

When it is over in a hydrogen-bomb-like explosion — you see, we didn't invent the H-bomb — Tane is happy like a child because he has found a new game. He takes his organ back of course, but every time She wants to borrow it from him, he lends it to her gladly. And so began the lending-borrowing game now popular not only between Tanes and Shes but between Tanes and Tanes, and Shes and Shes.

Soon Woman she gives birth to another She who in time becomes more beautiful than her mother. Now, as all long-married couples know (but won't tell you), the lend-lease-borrow-barter game gets boring. One needs variety in the ways of lending and borrowing and in the partners one plays the game with. So Tane he looks for variety with his daughter.

One night Woman hears her adulterous mate mating with her other self, so to speak biblically. She is jealous and horrified. (Incest is no laughing matter!) So she flees to the underworld, and is given legal permission by the gods to return to earth and destroy all the fruit of Tane and his daughter's incestuous but highly enjoyable union. She insists that the gods must give her god-status and a title befitting that rank. So they deify her as 'Hine-nui-te-Po'. Now you know that we are the manufactured products of Tane's incestuous organ stirring his own daughter's cream, so to praise New Zealand's main industry. But Tane's incest also led to man's death, to our own death.

Now Maui he decides one fine day to challenge Hine-nui-te-Po. He asks his friends the fantails to come with him and witness his humiliation of the death-goddess.

Hine, who is a giantess, is asleep on the horizon when Maui and his fantails find her. Maui tells his friends that he is going to enter Hine's womanhood — to speak delicately — and come out her mouth. (Human biology was one of Maui's failing subjects at university.) Before he begins his juicy journey he instructs his feathered friends to keep silent or Hine will wake and then there will be no more Maui. However, when Maui is inside, the fantails giggle because it is all so funny.

The girl was laughing so uproariously that he stopped talking. She came over, sat on his lap with her arms round his neck, and pleaded with him to finish.

And Hine-nui-te-Po she woke up and found him in there. And she crossed her legs and thus ended man's quest for immortality, he said slowly. She laughed into his neck.

Gazing into her eyes, he said, 'Am I forgiven now?' She nodded repeatedly and started to unzip his jeans. 'Promise you won't cross your legs and end my quest for immortality,' he said.

'I love you,' she whispered.

20

It took them only thirty minutes to reach the last town before they crossed the southern half of the Volcanic Plateau to Lake Taupo, where she said they could stay in her family's bach and spend a few days fishing. There would be no more towns before Taupo so they took the van to the nearest garage and asked them to check the tyres and brakes and fill the tank. Then they went to look for a place to eat.

It was just seven in the morning. In the main street there were only a few people and cars. A small milk bar was open.

The woman behind the counter was Maori. She was a small thin woman with a severe face, thick lips, and beaked nose. Her short hair was sprinkled with grey. She scrutinised them closely as they approached the counter. They deliberately pressed right up against it and returned her unnerving stare without saying anything.

The woman smiled unexpectedly and asked, 'What can I *do* you for?' They glanced at each other, not knowing how to take her unusual question. The woman burst out laughing, short staccato laughs.

'You can do us for a good breakfast,' the girl said. The woman stopped laughing at once, eyes still wild with merriment, and, noticing the amusement on the girl's face, burst out laughing again. He saw that two of her front teeth were missing. 'Do us some tea, bacon, eggs, toast, and don't forget the large sausages. Fry them until they're lusciously brown,' the girl added.

Laughing still, the woman turned and disappeared through the door behind her. They heard her talking to someone. Now and then she laughed.

They went and sat at a table near the front window.

'Strange woman,' he said.

She reached over, tapped his left cheek, and said, 'Still suspicious of Maoris, eh?'

'No, it's just that — well, what a thing to say to two strangers: "What can I do you for?" What kind of introduction do you call that?'

'It's the best introduction I've ever heard.' She laughed softly.' "What can I do you for?" What a beautiful way to begin the day!'

The woman returned and sat down beside him. He edged away. She told them the food would be ready soon. She introduced herself and started chatting to the girl. She fired a question at him periodically, and jabbed him in the ribs with her elbow every time she laughed (which was often). He didn't join in the conversation.

'You two fellas married?' the woman asked suddenly.

'Sort of,' the girl replied.

'I like that,' the woman said, her frail bony body shaking with laughter. 'I like that!' Turning to him, she jabbed him in the ribs again and said, 'You're a lucky fella. You've got a comedian for a missus.'

He relaxed and laughed with them. The woman talked about the town. He grew bored with her chatter.

'You're not a hori, are you, fella?' the woman asked. He shook his head.

'I can tell every time,' she said, more to the girl than to him.

'How?' the girl asked.

The woman looked at him and winked. 'Hell, he don't look like a hori. He's too serious. We horis, we laugh and joke all the time. . . .' As she talked, describing the very myths about Maoris that he had once believed, he felt a numbing sense of disappointment. Then he remembered that his mother talked about Samoa and Samoans the same way, but he pushed the thought out of his mind. The

104

woman paused. 'Where you from, boy?' she asked.

He was surprised he didn't mind at all being called boy. The woman, he concluded, was one of his kind. Two weeks before, in the city, he would have reacted violently to her calling him boy. 'Samoa,' he replied.

'Samoa, eh? You're a coconut then?'

'Yes,' he said.

From the kitchen a man called to the woman that the food was ready. She got some cutlery, plates, and cups from the counter and laid them on the table, all the time talking about a Samoan family she knew in Auckland. When the man called again she went and got the tray of food. As they ate she continued talking to them. Other customers entered but she ignored them. She called to the man — her husband, she said — to come and serve them. They got up to leave. She refused to let them pay for their meal. She accompanied them to the door.

He looked at her husband for the first time. He was pakeha. A thick-set, bald-headed man who was busy straightening the shelves behind the shop counter. He looked away and followed the woman and the girl out to the footpath.

'Thank you,' he said.

'It's only money,' the woman said. 'And it's his money.' She shook his hand. 'You take care of this girl now.'

'Thank you for doing us,' the girl said.

The woman clapped her hands and laughed again. Some of the people passing by looked at her disapprovingly. 'The bloody trouble with this one-horse town,' she said, loud enough for the people to hear, 'is that it's too respectable. What do you expect from the army though but one-shot privates and clumsy sergeants.' Her husband called to her to come in.

'He's a retired one-shot fella too,' she said. Her gaiety was gone. 'Remain sort of married,' she said. 'And don't have kids. Keep on being hippies.'

She hurried back into the shop.

As they walked to the garage to collect the van, they laughed about her last remark.

21

The van sang as it chased the road spinning away before
them into steep gullies and narrow steel bridges, then up
again across low hills covered with tussock, manuka, and
fern. The line of telegraph posts beside the road reminded
him of crucifixes set up against the grey sky. The rain had
stopped. The girl was driving.

As he observed the desolately bleak landscape, he felt as
if the van was being sucked further and further into the
shell of a huge silence. Why was it that he was always
attracted to desolate places, he wondered. To places like
this plateau, fashioned by volcanic eruptions, weighed
down by the sky wild with the threat of rain and lightning,
scarred by rivers to expose wounds of red volcanic soils
which bled in the rain, covered over wide areas by thick
volcanic ash, with everywhere protruding outcrops of lava
rock, like clenched fists threatening the sky? Perhaps it was
because such places reflected the truth of the human heart.

She looked relaxed as she drove deeper into the Plateau.
He allowed the silence to enter the pores of his thoughts
and fill the cell he lived in, with a contented, all-accepting
joy. She asked him if he knew what the road they were on
was popularly called. He shook his head.

'The Desert Road,' she said.

Shortly after, the centre of the Plateau loomed up
abruptly: three active volcanoes of black rock and ash,
capped with snow, cloud, and billowing smoke. Tongariro,
Ruapehu, Ngauruhoe. He remembered reading about the
mountains and the legendary tohunga, Ngatoroirangi, who

had first explored the region and given it name, form, and shape. The legend said that Ngatoroirangi populated the hills with the patupaiarehe, the fairy people. As he explored the waterless valleys, he stamped his feet into the ground, and lakes and springs and streams broke from the stony earth. The region was his, and to give it a name he climbed one of the three mountains. He took his slave girl, Auruhoe, with him.

Surveying the area from the summit, he was so struck by its awesome beauty that he forgot Auruhoe and the bitter cold snaring his body. The girl began to die in the snow. When he realised their danger he called to his sisters in Hawaiki, ancestral home of the Maoris, to save them. To him they sent the sacred fire which broke out through the centre of the North Island, creating hot springs and geysers in Wairakei, Rotorua, and Taupo. Then the fire burst up out of the three mountains and saved Ngatoroirangi by warming his body. But it came too late to save Auruhoe.

Ngatoroirangi fed her body to the sacred fire in one of the peaks and called that peak Ngauruhoe after her. The mountain from which he had appealed to his sisters, he named Tongariro.

Until the pakeha came to New Zealand, the area which the old tohunga had fashioned was tapu to the Maori people.

'There it is!' she said. He broke from the net of his thoughts and saw the lake.

They were travelling downhill through a shallow gorge which widened as they neared the lake. The land was getting greener and there were trees — eucalyptus and gum — and the beginnings of paddocks. They turned left and followed the shore of the lake which pulled away to the west, north, and south, until it was a low wall of haze and dull grey hills.

Occasionally they passed farm houses, more like shacks than houses, set well away from the road under trees behind broken-down fences. In some of the small bays, under trees near narrow beaches, were parked caravans surrounded by tents. On the nearest section of the lake there were a few rowing-boats with fishermen on them. The light had grown stronger and the grey was vanishing from the sky. Soon they were on the outskirts of Taupo township.

'All the Plateau needs to make it fertile pasture land, good farm country, is cobalt,' she said. He looked at her. All he could see in his mind was a sea of lush grass creeping across the Plateau, suffocating even the bare lava rock outcrops and surging up the three mountains to smother the sky and the dazzling image of the tohunga, Ngatoroirangi.

'All is grass,' he tried to joke.

'And dairy cows,' she said.

There was need of desolate places, deserts, tapu areas, he thought, where the mind and heart could find solitude — the sacred fire that warmed and made the self whole again.

They stayed in her family's bach by the lake for nearly a week. Before he saw the bach he had imagined it to be a shack used by campers. But it was a smaller version of her family home in the city, with hot and cold water, electricity, expensive furniture, and all the other comforts of a wealthy home. It was surrounded by lawns, flower gardens, and willow trees. She told him that a woman came once a week to clean the house; there was also a gardener. She had written to them to take a week's holiday.

Every morning she woke him early and they went fishing for trout in a light speedboat which belonged to her father. She taught him how to use a fishing rod. After he had caught a few trout he lost interest in fishing and spent the rest of the time watching her as she fished. Sometimes he lay down in the bow and went to sleep. Their last time out they made love as the boat drifted. They returned to the house and showered together.

They were leaving the shower when they heard someone knocking at the front door. She hurriedly wrapped a beach towel round herself, told him to hide in the bedroom, and went down the stairs before he could say anything. He heard her take the visitors into the sitting room downstairs. He could make out the voices of a man and a woman. It was obvious that she knew the people very well.

As he dressed he realised he was angry.

He opened one of the bedroom windows quietly, slid down on to the concrete overhang, and jumped down to the lawn.

She was ashamed of him, he thought, as he walked into town. He went into the first pub he found.

He bought a jug of beer, took it to the far corner, put it on the windowsill, and started drinking, his back turned to the bar. He finished the jug quickly, bought another one, finished that, and felt less angry. It was early afternoon and there were only a few customers in the pub. Three old men, drowsy with drink, sat near the front door at the one table. Dressed in dark sports coats, they reminded him of magpies gossiping quietly. Up against the bar stood four other men; they looked like farmers. On the opposite wall, above the bar, was nailed the stuffed head of a deer; its antlers coated with dust.

When he went up to buy his fourth jug, the barman, a rotund hairy man with nicotine-stained teeth, asked him if he was new in town. He nodded. As the barman refilled his jug, he remarked that Taupo was a nice town — good trout-fishing, the best in the world. Was he staying with relatives, the barman asked, adding that he knew all the important Maori families in the area. He shook his head. Maoris were terrific drinkers but there was no danger of them becoming alcoholics, the barman said.

About an hour later he was, so he told himself, floating, floating and relaxed and to hell with her. The pub had filled gradually during the afternoon, but he didn't take much notice of the other people.

For a moment he couldn't believe that someone had placed another jug of beer on the sill. It was *his* windowsill.

'May I join you, man?'

He wheeled to refuse, saw who it was, and nodded.

'Thanks, mate,' the Maori said, pouring himself a glass of beer. 'Cheers!' They raised glasses and drained them. 'Good stuff, great stuff!' sighed the Maori, wiping his mouth with the back of his hand.

They introduced themselves.

'Been drinking long?' the Maori asked.

'Had quite a few,' he said. 'Come on, drink up and I'll get some more.'

They finished their jugs quickly. He reached up to get the empty jugs but his friend (that was how he now thought of the other man) said, 'I'll get them. I live here.'

As they drank and talked, his friend reminded him more and more of his brother — he had the same open honesty and joviality. They were built the same way too: slightly short of six feet, thick, heavily muscled. Built low to the ground, feet planted squarely in the earth's gut, his brother had once described himself, boasting that he lived through the pores of his flesh. *You* can't accept people and things for what they are, his brother had accused him. You've become a fair-dinkum Kiwi.

Occasionally, as they talked, his friend called over some of his friends. Most of them were Maoris. Two pakeha youths joined them. Someone got a table from somewhere and they loaded it with jugs. Every time the jugs were empty someone had them filled. It was as if he was back in the city, drinking with a group of Samoans. He forgot the girl.

'Let's get some grog and have a grog-up at my place,' his friend said. The others agreed readily. 'Show your dough then.' They fished out money and stuffed it into his hands. 'Hey, fellas, there's going to be enough piss to drown my old man's house!' He sent the three youngest youths with the money to buy the beer.

Darkness had fallen when they rolled out of the pub. Everyone was talking loudly and one of the pakeha youths was singing at the top of his voice. No one on the street took any notice of them; they seemed used to it.

A red pickup truck, landscaped with dents, screeched to

a halt in front of them. In it were the youths who had gone to get the beer.

'Hey, what you get?' someone asked.

'A keg, twenty flagons, and lots of courage,' the driver said. ,

'You seen Mohammed Ali in town today?'

'Yeah, man, right here!' the driver declared, flexing his left arm through the window of the pickup. Everyone laughed as they piled on to the back.

The pickup roared drunkenly and shot off towards the lake and out of town into the darkness.

They started singing and passing a flagon round.

'Hey, you greedy bastards!' the driver called. 'How 'bout some piss for us fellas?' They handed him a flagon.

By the time they reached his friend's home, four empty flagons had been thrown out to smash on the road.

Before the others had joined them at the pub, his friend had told him that he lived with his parents just out of town. They had a small farm, about thirty acres. Over the years all his older brothers and sisters had shifted to live in the main cities. He'd stayed behind to look after his parents who were both quite old. (Anyway he didn't like cities.) Some of his nieces and nephews and cousins lived with them.

The farm wasn't much — a few sheep and cows, some chickens and pigs; enough to feed the family. He worked as a shearer during the season. In the off-season, when he had little to do on the farm, he spent most of his time fishing on the lake. He sometimes worked in town driving a truck. He'd once tried living in Auckland with his oldest brother, but he'd been gaoled for a week for brawling in a pub. After that he'd returned to Taupo.

Most of his school cobbers lived in Auckland now. They were nearly all married, lived in state houses, and had steady jobs. He wished he could be like them. One of his best mates was in Mount Eden gaol for life: he'd fallen for a pakeha dame, and one night when he was sozzled he'd strangled her because she was getting it from another joker. His other cobbers visited Taupo now and again. He avoided them as much as possible. They made him feel small; they were much more educated than him. A few of them he didn't like any more. They were bloody condescending, especially the jokers who'd been to university. They were so bloody full of themselves, full of pakeha flab, from their over-educated skulls to their toenails. One of the beggars, a high-up civil servant, always talked about 'integration' and family planning. He reckoned — and this was God's truth — that the proper-sized family for a country like New Zealand was two to three kids. (All fucken flab, his friend had laughed.) The sorry beggar was so whitewashed. He'd asked him to spell 'integration', meaning it as a joke, but the poor sod had gone right ahead and spelt it three times. He even went on to say that for the hori — and the shit used that word — that for the hori to make it in Kiwi society, he had to keep good health standards: clean houses, lavs, ears, toenails, teeth, and minds; the hori had to get a good education, learn a trade; the hori had to stop boozing all his money away, learn to save it for a rainy day, use it on his missus and kids; the hori had to obey the laws, stop behaving uncivilised, stop living in overcrowded homes, stop laughing loudly, stop fornicating freely and stop calling one another horis.

They'd laughed about it; then his friend had asked him where he was from. He said he was from Wellington so he must be full of flab. But he wasn't in love with most pakehas, or integration, or steady jobs and clean minds. He added that he was Samoan and went to university, bastion of flab. They'd laughed some more.

The next day he could remember few details of the party that all the neighbours had come to. Just the beautiful abandonment, the dancing and singing, and one huge Maori wanting a fight with him because he was a Samoan, a coconut, and the man hated coconuts because they'd worked him over in an Auckland pub. His friend had stopped the man by telling him he was just a stupid black bastard; and everyone had ended up laughing about it. He could remember vaguely that he'd blacked out in the late hours of the morning while demonstrating the Cook Island drum dance, which he'd learnt at church socials.

He woke up just before noon and had lunch with his friend and his family. They drove him to the bach. He said goodbye. They told him to come and stay with them any time he wanted to. He waved to them as they drove off. The children waved back. He watched the car until it disappeared.

As he walked up the drive to the front door of the bach, he felt alone again, as if he'd just farewelled friends he would never see again.

He knocked on the door. She opened it. He looked at her; she looked at him. He wasn't angry with her any more, but he sensed she was angry with him. He didn't want her to ask him where he'd been; it would force him into asking her why she hadn't wanted him to meet the people who'd visited the house the day before, and there would be an argument and they'd say things they would both regret.

He walked past her into the sitting room and lay down on the settee. She came and sat in the armchair opposite him. He refused to go to her; he wanted her to come to him.

'Well?' she asked.

'I was at a party,' he said. He felt very tired.

'Hell, and there I was — up all last night, worrying myself sick,' she said. 'Couldn't you have rung me?'

'Forgot about it,' he said. 'There's no phone here anyway.'

'You forgot about it? Shit! What kind of statement's that?'

He sat up and looked at her. 'I met these fellows and they took me to a party.'

'Couldn't you have taken me along?'

'I just forgot about it; let's leave it at that.'

She looked away. 'Was it a good party?'

'Yes, I enjoyed it.' He didn't want to tell her any more about it; she didn't own him.

'I went next door and rang the police and the hospital,' she said. 'And I suppose you met some bloody women there?'

'Yes,' he said. 'Anyway I don't have to tell you everything I do. You never tell me everything.'

'And what the hell does that mean?' She got up, came over, and glared down at him.

'Let's stop before we say things we don't really mean,' he said.

'No. I want you to bloody well tell me what you meant by that shit of a remark you made!'

Looking up at her, he said, 'Okay, if that's the way you want it.'

'That's the way I want it!'

'Okay, why did you hide me away from those friends of yours?'

'When?'

'Yesterday. And don't give me that forgetting act.' It was almost as if the party hadn't happened, as if he was still going to that pub, telling himself she was ashamed of him. She looked away from him. 'Go on, tell me!'

'I simply forgot about you. I was going to introduce you to them later on.'

'Don't give me that shit!' He waited for her to reply; she didn't. 'So you didn't want your lily-white friends to see your coconut boyfriend, eh?'

'That's not fair,' she said.

'What *is* fair then? I have to know!'

'I didn't want them to hurt you,' she said.

'What a load of crap!'

On the verge of tears, she said, 'They're not my friends. They belong to my bloody parents. And you don't know what they're like. I just didn't want you to be hurt by them. Believe me.'

'I don't believe you,' he said slowly. He went into the kitchen, got a glass of ice-cold milk, and came and stood beside her, drinking it.

She wheeled and ran up the stairs into the bedroom. He followed her.

She stood at the window, looking out at the lake. Caught in the bright light of the hot afternoon sun, she looked brittle, very vulnerable. He stopped in the doorway and watched her.

'And I suppose you thoroughly enjoyed fucking one of those women last night, and punishing me in your mind while you fucked her?' she said, trying to wrest control of the argument away from him.

'I didn't,' he said, angrier now, knowing that she was on the attack again.

Turning slowly to face him, she said, *'I don't believe you.'*

'I don't give a damn if you believe me or not!' He was nearly shouting. 'Anyway, even if I did do what you're accusing me of, I don't care what you think about it!' She turned and looked out at the lake. 'What about you?'

'Yes, what about me?' she asked, deliberately sounding as if she was bored with the whole thing.

'What about all those white bastards who had a good time with you?' Now it was all out in the open. The dark thing that had been troubling him ever since he became involved with her was out there confronting them both.

'What about them?' she said, still trying to sound casual. He didn't reply; he was in control of the argument again. 'What about them?' she repeated, turning to face him. He didn't answer. 'What was I supposed to do before you came along? Masturbate myself to death and remain a bloody virgin? You make me laugh. You're supposed to be Polynesian, fellow. Not a pure white pakeha puritan. Or didn't you know that, fellow? Polynesians are supposed to believe in free love; they're supposed to practise fucking all round!'

'That's enough!' he said, moving slowly towards her.

'You started it,' she said. 'Now I'm going to finish it. It hurts really bad, doesn't it? Hurts you to think that some pakeha enjoyed me sexually, doesn't it? That it was a pakeha who robbed me of my cherry? Well, just think about it again. See it now in your mind? Me, the only pakeha bitch you've ever allowed yourself to fall for, panting and moaning and groaning and loving it all under some virile pakeha?'

He hit her. She spun away from him and slammed into the wall behind her. She stood there, hands clutching her bleeding mouth, watching him as he moved towards her. He hit her again. Her head thumped against the wall. She started to cry, but swallowed it back.

He tore her clothes from her. She didn't resist him. He pushed her on to the bed. He pushed her legs apart and started making love to her. She tolerated him.

'You love me, don't you?' he asked. She turned her face away from him. 'I'm the only man you've ever loved. You *must* love me!'

She put her arms round him.

I'm sorry, she said.

So am I. It's good that it's all out in the open though.

What do you mean?

You know, about all those other men.

Yes.

Now we can see each other more clearly.

One more mirror shattered.

Yes. And what do I look like now?

More beautiful.

And more vulnerable.

And me?

Very small and limp and beautifully helpless. And I do love you more, I think.

I think I love you too. More so now. I was too scared to admit it to myself.

We sound like clichés in a pop song, don't we?

Yes, like in the romance comics.

But what can we use instead of the word 'love'?

Aroha? Alofa?

You are again strong with aroha.

And you are warm and moist and overflowing with alofa.

22

If love is the painful, joyous, frightening feeling that I need to be consoled by you and only you; and if I want so much to console you, then I do love you.

23

He was in the fifth form, preparing to sit his School Certificate. After the mid-year exams he tried to hide his report from his parents, but one evening after family prayers his father asked to see it. He got it from his bedroom and handed it to his father.

He unfolded it carefully and gave it back to him to translate into Samoan for all of them. He thought of translating it to suit what his parents wanted to hear. But he didn't; he translated it truthfully.

His mother congratulated him, promised him a new pair of long trousers, and then went to fix their dinner. His brother, who was now working, called him 'a brainy native'; his father congratulated him with a big smile, but then asked if the subjects he was studying would allow him to take a medical degree. This was what he had been trying to avoid. When he first started high school he had promised his father he would become a doctor; a healer, as his father called it.

He pretended he hadn't heard the question and started joking with his brother. His father asked him again.

'I'm ... I'm sorry,' he began apologetically, hoping in this way to ease the pain he sensed his father would feel.

His father told him to sit down. He said, 'You know I don't understand very much about this education you are having, so please explain to me why the subjects you are studying won't make you a doctor.'

He glanced at his brother who looked away. 'I'm

studying history,' he began slowly, 'and geography and maths and English and general science.'

'Now explain why those are not suitable preparation for becoming a doctor,' his father said.

'I need to take other subjects.' He looked at the floor.

'Such as?'

'Physics, chemistry, biology.'

'And why aren't you taking them?'

He hesitated, refused to seek refuge in tears, and said, 'Because I'm no good at them.' He looked at his father and saw pain, disappointment, anger. 'I'm doing very well at school, Papa,' he insisted.

'But you have disobeyed me,' his father said.

'I'm . . . I'm . . . .' he began to say, but his father got up and went into the hall. The front door opened and slammed and he heard his father walking up the footpath into the darkness.

At dinner that night, without his father, he told his mother what had happened.

'Your father,' she said, 'is just terribly disappointed. He is facing the end of one of his cherished hopes. It is not your fault.'

When he had done his homework he went into the sitting room and waited for his father to return. When his father entered the room, he began to apologise to him but his father told him not to. The room was cold but he didn't feel it because he sensed that his father wasn't angry with him any more.

His father explained that he had walked the city streets for a long time that night, thinking about many things, and indulging in self-pity. He was an ignorant man, his father said. He had only been to the pastor's school where he had learnt to read and write Samoan. In Samoa he had observed the changes taking place and had concluded that only people educated the papalagi way would have a good future in Samoa. That was the main reason he had brought them to New Zealand.

While he walked the streets he had finally admitted to himself that it was unfair of him to try to live out his hopes through his children; they had dreams of their own. With that admission, he had come to accept his son's wish not to be a doctor. It was painfully difficult for him to do so, he continued, because, by accepting it, he was denying the fulfilment of a family tradition which he himself had failed to achieve.

In the history of their family, he said, the youngest son had always been trained to be a healer; his father had been the last of that line. Staring fixedly at his trembling hands, his father admitted that he had failed to become a healer. He confessed that this was why he had wanted his youngest son to become a doctor. He owed it to their family, both living and dead. To end the tradition would be a rejection of God's most precious gift to their family — the gift of healing.

'But I have to accept,' his father said with a sigh. 'All is well.' He paused and then said, 'We owe you and your brother to the healing powers of a papalagi doctor. He cured your mother's barrenness.'

His son looked away.

'Some day you too will have to accept something that will break your heart,' his father said. 'Not because you want to accept it, but because you won't be able to do anything to change it.'

PART II

24

She gave him the address of the party over the phone. She sounded drunk and he could barely hear her above the noise of the party. 'Come find me!' she said, and put the phone down before he could say anything.

He rang for a taxi and drove to the house which was in one of the streets above the university, near the cable-car terminus. The night was chilly, a stiff wind was blowing in from the south, and the black starless sky echoed the fear he felt: for the first real time, he was confronted with the fact that he could lose her.

The front door of the house was made of thick glass through which he could see the crowded hall. People were sitting on the windowsills, and the house trembled with rock music and laughter and conversation. As he went up the steps he could tell it wasn't a student party: most of the people he could see were expensively and conservatively dressed — the friends she had said she never wanted him to meet because they would hurt him. Why was she forcing him to meet them now?

Some people were leaning against the front door. He hesitated — no one had seen him yet — and then knocked. A girl turned, looked at him, and tried to open the door. It was locked. She called to someone in the sitting room.

'Who is it?' he heard a man shout back. The girl and her three male companions turned and looked at him.

'An Islander I think,' the girl replied.

A short thickset man came out of the sitting room and pushed his way to the door. He unlocked it, half-opened it, and — with his hand still clutching the handle — peered coldly at him, and said, 'Yes?' The people beside the man watched.

'May I come in?' he replied. The man didn't move.

'Were you invited?' the man asked. He said that the girl had invited him. 'Wait here,' the man said, and returned to the sitting room.

The people in the doorway looked away from him and went on talking. He waited.

The man returned and beckoned to him to come in. He followed the man through the crowded hall into the sitting room.

The expensively large room was not as crowded as he had wanted it to be. There were only a few couples dancing; other people were scattered round the room in small groups. Empty spaces gaped at him.

The man left him stranded a few paces inside the doorway and went off. He sensed the hostility; he had been through it before, but usually there had been some people who had welcomed him quickly. The girl would come and he would be able to cope. He couldn't see her anywhere. He had to manage alone.

There was a luxurious bar at the far side of the room. When the record ended and the dancers began to disperse, he went over to it. The people round the bar parted and let him through.

'Yes?' the man behind the bar said; he was obviously the host.

'May I have a beer?' he said.

The man was tall and muscular, deeply tanned by the sun, with short-cropped blond hair and cold blue eyes. A rugby player or a surfie, he thought; wealthy and used to money, the admired centre of the group at the party; the man he would have to challenge if he wanted the girl back.

The man got a glass, opened a bottle of beer, and put the glass and bottle in front of him. He filled his glass, raised it towards the man, and said, 'Cheers!' He caught a flicker of contempt in the man's eyes. He emptied the beer down his throat. 'Great,' he said. He could take the man behind the bar.

The music started again and many of the couples round the bar went off to dance. He refilled his glass, the host watching him all the time, sat down on the nearest bar-stool, and turned his back to the host.

The girl came into the room with a middle-aged accountant he had once seen her talking to at university. He had his arm round her shoulders; her head nestled into his shoulder. When they reached the middle of the floor, she wound her arms round his neck and they danced slowly, tightly. She refused to look over at him.

He turned to the man behind the bar. 'Another beer?' he asked.

'Beautiful, isn't she?' the man said, looking at the girl, and opening another bottle for him. 'Known her well for a long time. Seems she's got another boyfriend now though.' He came from behind the bar. 'Must have a dance with her.' The man motioned to go to the girl, stopped, turned to him, and said: 'You want to meet her? She really likes Islanders. Probably because coconuts are supposed to be big where we fellows should be big.'

He refused to be baited; he would wait. He winked at the man and continued drinking. The man went over and danced with the girl. It was almost impossible for him not to look at the girl and the man as they danced and caressed each other. But he was completely sure of himself again.

The music stopped. He waited. The man steered the girl over to him. When she looked up at him, he knew she wasn't as drunk as she appeared to be.

'Who's your handsome friend?' the girl asked the man, who had his arm round her.

The man looked at him. 'Hey, what's your name? I've forgotten it.' The music started again.

Ignoring the man's question, he reached over, grasped the girl's hand and said, 'May I?' He began to pull her towards the dance-floor.

'No!' she said, stepping away from him. The people round the bar watched them.

'It seems, fellow, that the lady doesn't want to dance with you,' the man said.

He looked at her; she smiled at him. Come find me, she had pleaded over the phone. Now he thought he understood what she meant.

'Are you leaving with me?' he asked her.

'She's not leaving with anyone,' the man said.

He looked at the man. It was all so familiar (and ridiculous), he thought. The type of New Zealand man he'd always disliked, attempting to prove his masculinity in public; the rugby player and surfie who, suffering from fear of his own inadequacies as a male, believed the racist myth of black virility, and who was now trying to convince himself (and his friends) that the myth wasn't true. The whole history of the pakeha had been cursed with this fear, and the Maoris and other minority groups had to pay for it. All pakeha women who went out with Polynesians and blacks were considered nymphomaniacs after the supersized whang. Conversely, all pakeha men who took out Polynesian women were after the expert fuck.

In silence he started to walk towards the door leading to the hall.

'Aren't you going to fight him?' the girl called. He stopped for a moment, made up his mind, and went into the hall. 'Coward!' he heard her shout as he opened the front door.

He walked slowly along the winding street leading down to the university. He didn't feel the cold: his anger kept him warm.

He soon heard her running after him.

She wrenched him round to face her. 'You bastard, bastard, bastard!' she cried, slapping his face again and again. He stood, eyes clenched tightly, fists locked in the pockets of his thick leather jacket, and did nothing. She stopped slapping him and burst into tears.

He embraced her and, when she stopped crying, steered her down the street. The crisp air smelt of rain.

'Why didn't you beat up that smug shit?' she asked. 'I wanted you to.' He didn't reply. 'Now they're more

convinced than ever that all Islanders and Maoris are
bloody cowards.'

'I'm too chicken-hearted to fight over a woman,' he said.
'You wanted me to prove to them that your coconut
boyfriend is as good as they are, didn't you?'

'No, that's not true.'

'Before I met you I would have broken him in front of
his friends. I would have enjoyed it.'

They walked in tense silence for a while.

'Why have you been avoiding me?' he asked finally.

'I wasn't avoiding you,' she said.

He stopped walking; she stopped too, and he held her
chin and turned her face towards him. 'Okay, I'll buy that
bull. But why the hell did you want to invite me to that
party with all your silly stupid rich friends? And don't tell
me you didn't to it deliberately.'

She didn't answer.

They went to the nearest stop and caught the cable car
down to the city. As they left the terminus she said she
wanted some coffee, and they went into the coffee bar in
the alleyway leading to the main street.

They had been back from their trip for over a month.

I'm sorry about the last two weeks. I didn't know what I
was doing and why I was deliberately hurting you.

It's okay. I'm glad you're back again.

They're stupid and silly, aren't they?

Who?

My so-called friends. After being away from them for
so long, I wanted to go back to them; find out if I was still
like them. Or whether being with you had changed me for
the better. I found out tonight: they're a useless, heartless,
bigoted bunch. Too many empty pretensions, too much
money. And to think I was once like them.

But why did you want me there?

Maybe I wanted them to hurt you, punish you, for taking
me away from them and the senseless world I used to like
and feel comfortable in. Maybe I wanted you to hurt them
because they're the bloody types who make this shit of a

town tick, and who are down on all people with different skin pigmentation. . . . Why didn't you beat up that stupid arrogant bastard?

He was the one, wasn't he?

The one?

You know?

Yes, he was the one. I grew up with him. He's the son of my father's best friend. They always planned that we'd get hitched eventually. One day, when we were home from our exclusive boarding schools, we just decided to get the physical side of the plan inaugurated, and he took my cherry — to speak politely of something I'd lost millions of times in my frustrated mind in that sexless boarding school. I got bored with him by the time we finished high school. After three other fellows, I found myself back with him again for a few months. Got bored with him again, and had the others. Then you came along. Being Polynesian, I thought you'd be a quaint novelty, and here I am — miserably in bloody love with you.

And that accountant?

He was one of them. But, darling, I haven't been unfaithful to you since we first met. You believe me?

Yes.

I wanted you to really hurt him.

Who?

You know. I wanted you to make him bleed, hurt him badly for making love to me before I met you. Deep down I'm still a little puritan believer in a woman preserving her purity for the man she loves. I didn't love him. Didn't love the others either. Sometimes I thought I did. The so-called new morality is full of shit . . . . Know something, darling?

No.

I love you.

I love you too.

Do you know something else?

No.

I'm pregnant.

Are you sure?

Positive. Saw our family doctor twice. Had tests. I *am* pregnant. That's why I've been so bloody mixed-up for the last two weeks.

Why didn't you tell me earlier?

Because I wasn't sure what your reaction would be. . . . What *is* your real reaction?

I'm . . . I'm happy. Let's get married.

No!

He caught up to her at the end of the alleyway. She pulled away when he tried to hold her. For a long time they walked in silence towards the railway station, past gaping shop windows flooded with blaring orange light, oblivious of the people passing by like fish in some dimly opaque sea; the wind whistling. He remembered the first time they'd walked that way together, and how he had refused to help that man unconscious on the footpath; how he hadn't wanted to get too involved with her.

They sat on a bench, waiting for the train to arrive. There were only a few people on the platforms. Opposite them, across the first series of tracks, lay an old man, asleep on a bench. He wore a shabby brown overcoat; his wretchedly thin face, stubbled with grey, was turned upwards to the silver-bright flood of light from the platform ceiling; he looked as if he was dead. An empty whisky bottle lay on the bench beside his head. Curled up on the bench, the old man reminded him of a foetus, and then of that other old man at the rubbish dump — *Nazis? What is Nazis?*

She shifted over and pushed herself into his warm side. He asked her why she didn't want to get married. She said it was because, sooner or later, if they got married he would accuse her and their child of having forced him into an unwanted marriage; she didn't want their marriage to end up like her parents' marriage. He insisted that it wouldn't, that he loved her.

Perhaps it would be better for her to have an abortion; then they could get married, she said. He suddenly realised that he couldn't take his eyes off the old man on the opposite platform. Anyway, she said finally, she needed at least a week to think about it some more.

For you, she has become an extension of who and what you have grown into through knowing her. Without her, you would be much less than you are now. As you walk the main street of this city which, through loving her, you have learnt to accept, under the dark dome of this sky that covers this country which, through loving her, you have grown to know in all its moods and sickness and loneliness and joy and colours and cruelty, this is what your heart tells you. She is you; the very pores of your breath. Without her, this city, this country, would be a barren place of exile. And, as you walk further into the maze of this city, these grey walls and floors of concrete and steel and stone, you know that without her, the labyrinth would eventually turn you into stone, for modern cities are the new man-made deserts in which man traps himself and bleeds himself of all his rich warm fertile humanity and goodness.

Loving her and knowing to the frightened quick of your bones that you can now lose her, has made you fearfully aware for the first time of the impermanence of all things and the finality of life: that even love — the most precious feeling we can have for one another — can die or be destroyed. But you have no choice. You are committed totally, for love commits one totally to life and to death.

Why now do you suddenly think of Maui's fate? Of his death in the womanhood of Hine-nui-te-Po? Perhaps Maui was, after all, deeply in love with the death-goddess, and it was that love which made him wholly mortal and destroyed him.

Walk on. Walk home. Walk home slowly. She has left on the train. But you will see her tomorrow.

25

She stood on the back porch and observed her mother in the garden behind the house. She was watering her rose bushes from a fat watering can. Dressed in a black plastic raincoat, a white plastic hood, and pink rubber gloves, her mother looked like a nun as she moved slowly round the garden. The air was chilly, the sun caught behind a thick mattress of grey cloud. The roses didn't need watering.

The garden, immaculately without weeds, was about twenty yards wide and ten yards long. Immediately behind it a clay bank shot up sharply into hills. They had moved into the house ten years before; that decade had been, for her mother, the rose garden. A large glasshouse, which in the pale light reminded her of a butterfly cocoon made of eggshell, stood at the right-hand corner of the garden. Her mother spent much of her day in the glasshouse, safe from the rest of the world.

She gazed up at the hills yellow with gorse. She smelt smoke in the air. She saw her mother pause and look up at the hills for a frightened moment. Then her mother smiled, her wet raincoat glistening like the sleek hide of some strange sea creature.

The girl went along one of the concrete paths which criss-crossed the garden and asked her mother if she needed any help. Her mother shook her head and kept on working. (She guarded her garden jealously.)

Not knowing what else to do, the girl sat down on the bench behind her mother. For a breathless instant, as she gazed up into the sky, she felt as if it was sucking her up, up and away from the problem she didn't really want to confront her mother with.

'Why aren't you at your lecture?' her mother asked. She blinked and was back in the garden. She saw in the soggy rose bed at her mother's feet, an earthworm — pink like the colour of a new-born baby — wriggling up out of the earth.

'I'm not feeling well,' she said, closing her eyes, tasting a taint of nausea in her mouth.

'You should take something and stay in bed,' her mother said.

She had to say it then, had to try to pierce the black ominous raincoat, and talk with the woman who, when she was a child, had consoled her whenever she was in pain.

'He wants to marry me,' she said.

'Who does?' her mother asked, with her back still turned, still watering the roses.

She told her. 'And I want to marry him,' she added.

'Talk to your father about it. He'll know what to do.' her mother said, starting to walk towards the glasshouse.

The girl watched her. Her mother stopped in the doorway, turned, and called: 'He's dark, isn't he? Oh, why did you have to ruin my day?' Then she disappeared into the white, brittle cocoon.

For a stunned time the girl sat staring at the glasshouse, which, in her bitterness, reminded her of a mausoleum set in an expensive cemetery.

That night she heard her parents quarrelling in their bedroom. She wrapped a blanket round herself, went out and sat on the front lawn, and gazed down into the cold lights of Lower Hutt, and across the harbour to the city, imagining she was in the warmth of his bed, his love healing her and protecting the new life inside her from her parents and from what her mind, in the past weeks, had dictated she must do. The air and the darkness and the lights of the city and suburbs pressed in around her, breathing heavily, threateningly. It was as though the country itself didn't want her to have his child.

26

On Saturday afternoon, after he had mowed the front lawn and helped his mother weed her vegetable garden, his parents asked if he would take them to the pictures that night. He took them to see an Italian western, and they thoroughly enjoyed the flippantly gory killing. When they returned home, his mother made some cocoa; they sat in the sitting room in front of the electric heater, drinking it out of large tin mugs. His parents discussed the film enthusiastically. His mother was a devastating mimic, especially of western gunfighters. He wanted to escape to the solitude of his room, where he had spent the last few days thinking of the girl and of what had happened, but — caught in his parents' carefree laughter — he stayed in the sitting room and took part in the hilarious reconstruction of the film.

He finished his cocoa and got up to go.

'What is the matter?' asked his mother.

He glanced at her, shrugged his shoulders, and said, 'Nothing's the matter.'

'Sit down,' his father said. 'Now, what is worrying you?'

He didn't want to tell them; it wasn't the time yet. 'Just studying too hard, I think.'

'If that's all, just don't study for a few days,' his father said.

He caught his mother staring at him. She could always see into him, uncover most of his secrets, read his moods and thoughts. He cursed her silently. He got up to leave again.

'How is she?' his mother asked.

He refused to sit down again. 'Who?' he replied.

'You know who I mean,' she said.

'Oh, she's well.'

'You are still seeing her?' she asked. 'She hasn't visited us for over two weeks now.'

He looked at his father; he should protect him from her penetrating interrogation; he had always done so in the past. But the look on his father's face told him that he too wanted to know.

'Yes,' he said. 'Is there anything wrong in that?'

'No, there is nothing wrong in that. Sit down,' his father said. He sat down automatically, and when he realised he had sat down he grew more annoyed with them. He gazed sullenly at the floor.

'Now what is wrong between you and her?' his mother asked. He glanced at her. When he came home from the trip with the girl she had dismissed the whole thing with one simple question: Had he enjoyed it? He had said yes and was ready to tell her about the trip but she had started to discuss what he was going to do at university that term. Since then she had deliberately avoided talking about the trip, even when the girl visited them and she treated her like one of the family.

'There isn't anything wrong between us,' he said. 'Can't you leave it alone?'

'Don't talk to your mother like that,' his father cautioned him. 'We just don't want to see you unhappy.'

'I'm not unhappy,' he said. Why couldn't they stop treating him like a child, he suddenly found himself thinking. He wanted to shout at them to leave him alone, that he was now an adult and had a right to solitude and unhappiness and pain, and didn't need them any more to ease it; that his feeling and thoughts and suffering were not communal property. Not any more.

'Do you love her?' she asked.

'I want some privacy,' he heard himself say. He saw his parents look at each other. They just didn't understand what he meant. To them everything in the family was to be shared; pain was to be borne together by the family group. 'I want to be left alone with my own fears,' he tried to explain.

'You enjoy carrying your misery by yourself?' she asked, surprised.

'Put that way — yes.'

'But do you love her?' his father persisted.

'Yes,' he sighed. 'Yes, I love her.' Forgive me, he wanted to say, but didn't. There was nothing to be forgiven for. Loving a papalagi girl was not a crime, a sin, a betrayal of loyalty to his race, even though his mother and most Samoans saw it that way.

'Love her enough to want to marry her?' his father asked.

He looked at his mother. He didn't want to answer because he knew what her reaction would be: she would recall all the debts he owed her for the love and care she had lavished on him the whole of his life. Pressed, she would even recall the breath she had breathed into him. So he said nothing. He could hear them breathing, waiting.

'Answer your father's question,' she encouraged him. The bait was gentle; she sounded as if she would understand and accept. He knew that; but he also realised that he had to be honest with himself, to destroy her pretence finally, and be free from his childhood and the security of family.

So, gazing directly at her, he said: 'Yes, I want to marry her.'

The words punched home. She cringed visibly with every word, with every weight of the truth that he was now breaking away from her.

'No!' she exclaimed, refusing to accept the severance of the umbilical cord. 'She is papalagi. You cannot love her enough to want to marry her!'

'I have no choice,' he said. 'I love her more than anything else.'

'More than us?' she asked. He refused to answer. Bent forward in her armchair, her long black hair covering most of her face, arms clutched tightly across her belly, she rocked back and forth, weeping mutely, mourning.

He went to her and tried to embrace her. She pushed him away.

'Tell him he cannot do this to us,' she pleaded with his father. 'Tell him!'

'That's enough,' his father replied. He looked at his father but he looked away.

'He is *your* son. Order him not to marry her!' She was almost shouting.

'That is enough!' his father said.

The young man reached down again to embrace her, but she slapped his arms arms away. 'I curse the day you were born!' she shouted. 'My own son married to a palagi. My grandchildren to be half-castes. It cannot be!' Looking up at him, her eyes brimming with wild tears, she said, 'Do her parents want her to marry you?'

'I don't know,' he said.

'There, they don't want her to. All palagi discriminate against us.' She reached up and clutched his hands. 'Listen to me. She will destroy you. She won't fit into Samoa. Your own people will hold it against you for marrying a palagi. And . . . and her palagi parents hate you. Believe me!'

He pulled his hands out of her fierce grip and stumbled out of the room and out of the house into the empty night street.

His father caught up to him a short distance down the street, and put a comforting arm round his shoulders. They walked slowly. He wept quietly, trying to swallow the pain.

They found themselves in front of their church. They sat down on the church steps in the glow of the porch lights, and said nothing for a long time.

All the neighbouring houses were in darkness. Only the street lights shone, one-eyed crosses in the dark. He thought of eroded hills where nothing could grow, as he looked at the houses. And he thought of the many wives and husbands, both Polynesian and papalagi, who were asleep in their lonely rooms, wife separated from husband in cold beds, and dreaming fitful dreams of love in the succulent time of their youth which the years had turned into hygienic ruins, gutted silences, petty and lacerating quarrels of the bourgeois life, and the final refusal to utter the words, love, forgiveness. And he thought of her and vowed that their marriage would not die like that.

His father interrupted his thoughts. 'Your mother didn't mean what she said. She will come to accept whatever you decide.'

'I know,' he said. 'I didn't want to hurt her. But I had to tell her the truth.'

'I grew to love your mother,' his father said. 'That, I think, is the most permanent way between a man and a woman. You grow together.' He paused for a moment, chuckled, and asked, 'Have you been with many women?'

'A few,' he replied.

'Both palagi and Samoan?'

'Yes.'

'I've often wondered what it would be like.'

'What?'

'Being with a palagi woman. But I don't suppose they're any different from our own women. All women, the good women, they all heal a man's pain, like soothing ointment or the air of the morning. Is she like that?'

'Yes.'

'Then she is a good woman. Has she told you yet whether she wants to marry you?'

'Not yet. She wants me to give her time to think about it.'

'Then she cannot be sure.'

'It's not that,' he said.

'What is the matter then?'

He debated quickly. 'She is with child.'

'So you want to marry her because of that?'

'No.'

'So it is because you love her?'

'Yes.'

'Does she love you?'

'Yes. I think she does.'

'Are you sure?'

'Yes.'

'Then why does she want time to think about marrying you?'

'She wants to be sure that we are not getting married because of the child.'

'Then it is all right with me. I will talk to your mother.'

'Thank you.' He reached over and placed his hand on his father's shoulder. 'It must be difficult for you to say that. It may mean the end of your plans for us and our return to Samoa.'

'Yes, I have considered that. But it is your life too. And if she is a good woman, good for you and to you, she will give you a good life in Samoa. . . . But what if she decides not to marry you?'

27

Her mother came into the kitchen as she was drying the breakfast dishes, and began to search for something in the cupboards under the sink.

'He wants to talk to you,' her mother said.

She hung up the tea towel and asked, 'Who?'

Without looking at her, her mother said, 'Your father of course.'

'When?'

'Ten this morning I think he said.'

'Where?'

Her mother stood up. 'Have you seen my gardening gloves? I can't find them anywhere.'

'Where does he want to talk to me?'

'Oh, at his office.' Her mother opened the drawers under the cupboards, found her rubber gloves, and started to pull them on. The rubber smacked and snapped.

The girl wheeled to leave.

'Darling?' her mother said. She turned to her. 'Darling?' her mother repeated.

'Yes?' she pleaded.

Her mother looked down at her gloved hands. 'Nothing,' she murmured.

The girl almost ran out of the room.

She showered and dressed in her most rebellious clothes: scruffy jeans, thick leather sandals, a tight-fitting jersey, a wide leather belt studded with silver stars, and five bead necklaces. She brushed her long hair down over her shoulders and back.

Her father's office was in the top storey of a building belonging to his company. She took the lift. The lift operator, a pimply-faced youth with foul-smelling breath, talked to her about the weather and asked if he could take her to the pictures. You know, take a flick and have lots of fun afterwards, he said. The lift stopped and the door swept open.

She told him to keep hand-exercising his small gift furiously until it was man enough and then to ask her again. Keep pulling hard, she advised him, as she stepped out into the corridor. Bloody bitch of a hippie! she heard him call.

She went into the main office swinging her heavy leather handbag, and marched up the aisle between the rows of clerks, typists, and other office workers seated at their desks. Some of them recognised her and called hallo. Someone whistled. She waved; the man laughed. Just like a science laboratory, she thought. Polished, hygienic, orderly, all deodorised plastic — the modern minotaur's lair.

She flung open the door of the secretary's office and went in.

Her father's secretary, a tall, middle-aged woman, looked up but did not recognise her. She sat down opposite the woman, who said, 'What can I do for you?'

'I want to see the minotaur,' she replied. She almost laughed when the woman blinked behind her silver-edged glasses and said, 'Whom did you say?'

'Want to see my old man,' she said.

The woman smiled. 'Oh, I didn't recognise you in those clothes.' Then she was again the stern, efficient, officious secretary. 'You want to see him?'

'No, but he wants to see me.'

'He's got a very full schedule this morning. And he told me not to admit anyone who hasn't made an appointment.'

'For Christ's sake, I'm his only offspring. And he *did* want to see me.'

The woman ran her finger down the list of appointments. 'Oh, yes. You're down for ten o'clock.' She consulted her watch. 'And it's only nine o'clock now.'

She didn't wait for the secretary to say anything else. She got up, opened the door to her father's office and went in.

Blue carpet covered the floor of the spacious air-conditioned room. (Her father had sinus trouble and contracted hay fever easily.) A formidable circular mahogany desk occupied the centre of the room. Behind it sat her father. Directly behind him on the white wall was a hefty painting of the Crucifixion, set in a New Zealand landscape of dark green treeless hills. Three other landscape paintings by well-known artists hung on the other three walls.

He was reading through a thick folder of notes and hadn't heard her come in. She strolled over and sat down on one of the padded leather chairs in front of his desk.

She rarely visited his office. Whenever she was in it for any length of time, she had a dizzy feeling of panic, of being shut in a sound-proof box lost somewhere in the bottom of an ocean.

'I'm here,' she said.

He looked up, smiled, and shut the folder. 'You're early,' he said.

'Yes.' She stared at him.

He avoided looking at her. 'Now,' he said, as if he was starting an important business meeting, and stopped. She continued to scrutinise him. He glanced up at the ceiling, scratched his left ear, pushed his chair back, smoothed his hair down, pulled his chair towards his desk again, looked directly at her, and said: 'How are you feeling?'

'I'm okay,' she replied.

'Good. I've been worried about you, honey.' He turned his chair and gazed at the windows across the room. 'Your mother hasn't been feeling well lately. I think she's been working too hard in that garden of hers. I think I'll take her on a holiday this Christmas. Think that's a good idea, honey?' When she didn't reply, he said, 'Think I'll take her to the islands. The climate there would do her a lot of good.' He turned and faced her again. 'You want to come with us?'

'Where to?'

'The islands, honey.'

She shook her head. His eyes lit up hopefully. 'Does that mean you don't want to visit places like Samoa?'

'Not with you,' she said slowly. She could see him deliberately working himself into a rage. It was always his way.

'Now, why are you angry with me?' he said. It was more an accusation than a question. 'Have I said anything wrong?'

'No.'

'That isn't the way to speak to your father.' He was ready, good and angry and ready. 'Now what's this argument you started with your mother a few days ago?'

'I didn't start any argument,' she said. 'I just told her I wanted to get married.'

He switched immediately. He stood up and accused her of being dressed like a penniless hippie. Straight after their talk she was to go home, apologise to her mother, and put on some decent clothes, he said. He sat down again and started to talk about decency and respectability, based on honestly earned wealth. Without moral decency, physical decency, financial decency, you were nothing, he declared. Didn't she realise she was the heir to the position, wealth, power, and decent traditions of an ancient line of decent, honest people? Her grandparents had worked honestly and hard to hack something out of the wilderness, something worth-while and permanent to leave him and his brother and their children. He, in his own modest way, had added and was still adding to that heritage. He had won respect, admiration, envy. Now it was her turn to carry on that worthy family tradition. The modern generation had no guts, he said. If they had to live through a depression they would just fold up and die!

As he talked, verbally remoulding what he deemed to be old family traditions into a new sacred family mythology, purged of all the skeletons in the family cupboard, the oppressive feeling of panic welled up inside her again, and she realised that this panic was associated with a deep-rooted family guilt that she had inherited from a past inhabited by the ghosts of innocent people, both pakeha and Maori, whom her ancestors had destroyed. She had to exorcise those spirits.

'My grandfather was a thief,' she heard herself say. 'So were all those uncivilised, uncouth savages who came here from England!' Her father's voice suddenly stopped and she felt her panic leaving her. She gazed at him. He was fixed to his chair, like her grandfather enthroned in his wheelchair, a cripple. 'I've inherited blood and lies and fears and nightmares from you and all of them. And superstitions you call 'truths' — such as decency, respectability, progress, money, white racial superiority. It's all bull-shit, Daddy.'

He stood up slowly, turned his back on her, and gazed up at the painting on the wall behind his desk. She wanted to go to him, tell him she hadn't meant what she had said. It was so lonely this new-found feeling of freedom.

'Why did you sell the farm?' she asked after a minute.

He looked pale and very vulnerable when he turned. He would be truthful with her now. 'If you must know,' he said, 'I sold it because — because I felt I could never be myself if I didn't get rid of it. I preferred the money, it's easier to live with.' Gazing back at the painting on the wall he said, 'I also sold it because of her.'

'Grandmother?'

'No.'

'Then who?'

'A beautiful girl I used to know. Used to know and love. Please don't ask me about her. Allow me this one secret.' He tried to smile. 'It's the one beautiful ghost I prefer to live with by myself.' He bent his head and, staring at his hands, said, 'Enough for me to say, she was Maori and your grandparents forced me away from her. I didn't need much forcing. I convinced myself she would be a handicap to my career.'

She rushed over to him. He hesitated, then put his arms round her. 'I'm sorry,' she whispered.

'Everything's okay,' he said.

There was a knock on the door. He pushed her away gently and gave her his handkerchief. She was wiping her eyes when his secretary marched into the room.

'Yes, what is it?' he said.

'You have a board meeting now,' his secretary replied. He moved to go to his desk, stopped, and looked at his daughter. 'Shall I get out the appropriate file?' his secretary said, going towards the filing cabinet at the back of the room.

'No,' he said. 'No. Tell them to have the bloody meeting without me. I'll okay anything they agree on.'

His secretary glanced at him, then at his daughter, and left the room.

He told her that he had changed his hypocritical mind about her clothes, that she looked stunning, unusual. She laughed softly. But she should wear a bra, he added. She continued to laugh.

He sat for a minute in silence. 'Don't expect too much of me, girl,' he said finally. 'I'm too bloody old to change, to be what you want. We become creatures we never really mean to because of circumstances, our own selfishness, etc., etc., etc., and, of course, because of the little lies we tell ourselves.' He paused for a moment. 'If only I had it to start all over again.' He sighed. 'Anyway, I can't. And even if I could, I'd probably be what I am now. I wouldn't have it any other way — what would the RSA do without me?' He chuckled and winked at her. 'Have I been all that terrible as a father?' She shook her head. 'There you are!' He laughed and, reaching over, ruffled her hair. 'What will you do with all the money I'm going to curse you with?'

'Spend it as fast as possible,' she said.

'It'll kill you, but it'll be a helluva comfortable way of kicking the bucket.'

'Well, I'll give it away then.'

'No, you won't. You'll be giving away my blood and guts and brains . . . .'

'And genitals?' she said.

He laughed loudly. And for an hour or so they talked about the many camping trips they had been on in the past. They laughed and joked a lot as they talked.

He asked her what she was going to do for the rest of the day. She was going to buy some *decent* clothes and a bra, she said. They laughed about that too.

'Do you still want to marry that boy?' he asked.

'He isn't a "boy"'.

'I didn't mean it that way, honey. Or maybe I did mean it that way. Our quaint pakeha language is a way of life. Forgive me?' She nodded. 'Do you still want to marry him?'

'Yes, more than anything else.'

'He's poor. He won't be able to provide for you in the style you're accustomed to. And, honey, you're helluva spoilt. If he takes you back to the islands, you may find yourself living in a grass hut. The South Seas aren't what they're made out to be.'

'I know that.'

'And from what I've read and heard, they're very violent people.'

'Who's "they"?'

'They? Samoans. Almost every day you read about one of them being charged with assault.'

'Daddy, your racism is showing,' she said.

Her joke escaped him. 'I'm not a racist,' he said. 'I have many Maori friends.'

'Who?' she asked, and watched him scrambling to think of names.

'Well . . . well, I have two fellows working here. And that Reverend What's-his-name. And the anthropologist I met in Auckland last year. Now there's a really educated Maori.'

'Got any Samoan "friends"?' she asked, trying not to laugh.

'Honey, they're a new group in the country. I haven't

had a chance to meet many of them. Besides, we don't move in the same circles.' He stopped. She sensed that he was going to change tactics. 'By the way, what's he going to do?' he asked.

'Teach,' she said. 'I might as well tell you before you tell me that he won't make much money as a teacher. He won't be able to move in your circles either, even if he wanted to.'

'He doesn't want to?' He looked surprised.

'Will your friends, associates, and underlings let him?' she asked.

'I don't give a damn about them. They'll come round.'

'Well,' she said, 'he doesn't want to. And neither do I any more.'

'Be reasonable, honey. If he's to be my . . . .' He stopped, finding it difficult to say it, accept it.

'Say it,' she prompted him.

'Well, if he's to be my son-in-law. (Hell, why can't people be content with what they have!) If he's to be your husband, he's got to learn to live in my climate.'

'Why?'

'Because of the fact that he's my son-in-law!'

'Then you accept the fact that he's going to be your first and only son-in-law?'

He reached across the desk and clasped both her hands. 'Darling, don't make me do it.'

'Do what?' she asked.

'Make him my son-in-law,' he said.

'I'll be the one doing it, not you,' she said.

'So why do you want me to give my consent?' Another change in strategy.

'Because it's important to me,' she said.

'Why is it important?'

She moved quickly, right into the soft underbelly of his heart. 'Because it would prove to me that . . . that . . . .'

'Yes?' he encouraged her.

She turned her face away. 'That you love me.' He thought she was nearly in tears, but she was hiding her face so he wouldn't see that she was almost overcome with triumphant laughter.

His grip on her hands tightened protectively, and he said, 'Put that way, darling, I can't refuse, can I?' She looked at him and laughed. 'You damned unscrupulous scoundrel,' he said, and laughed with her.

She flung her arms round his neck.

Just before she left, he asked her to listen carefully to what he was going to say. He began by telling her what her marriage to a Samoan was going to do to her mother. She might not be able to face it, he said. It was a pity she didn't like coloured people. She couldn't help it; she was from a family who had never tried to understand other races. It wasn't really racism — it was just lack of understanding plus a fear of the unknown. It was much easier to get to know a white person than a person with a different coloured skin. You had something in common with another pakeha, a whole common cultural heritage. But, given time and a few beautiful grandchildren, her mother would forgive her. He would try to help her mother to understand by giving her the love he had failed to give her in the past. He would really try, he promised. Next year he might even retire and take her mother on a world trip to see all the places they, as a young married couple, had promised themselves they would see but never had. He would try to be kind and considerate and consoling, he promised his daughter, as he should have been but never had, because he'd been too busy building a bank vault round his soul.

She was convinced that he would keep some of the promises he was making. But she knew it was too late for him to save the woman he had married and helped to destroy. It was too late also for him to salvage the self he had mutilated over the years. Some of the wounds they had inflicted on each other would heal, but the deeper ones would continue to bleed and fester.

They needed to be loved, and she did love them more than they would ever know, but she had a life of her own to forge. A different kind of life. The man she loved would help to make it different, give it the meaning of all living things, alive with sap and constant self-renewal. Without him, she feared that her life would become like her parents' lives, haunted by the husks of visions and ideals they had bartered for a precarious bourgeois security and for the quick deodorised injection between splayed thighs once a week, then once a year. Then would come the cold menopause of the flesh and heart and soul, and the drift into a frigid religiosity and an over-riding fear of anything new and strange and fabulous. Without him and the love she felt for him, there would be just a slow turning into stone.

When her father had finished talking, she kissed him and got up to leave.

'Have you forgiven us?' he asked.

'For what?'

'For getting married because of you.' It was the first time he had ever admitted this to her.

'Yes, I always have,' she said. 'Before I go I have to tell you one more thing.' She paused and, gazing at him, said: 'I'm pregnant but I don't want to marry him because of that. I love him and I do want to be his wife, but I have to consult one more person before I tell him yes.'

'Who?' he asked.

'His mother. If she consents, I'll marry him immediately.'

'What if she doesn't?'

28

He would never know from her that she had consulted his
mother. She had done so one morning while he was at
university; they had talked for a long time. She respected
his mother and what she wanted her to do; she would obey
her and not tell him. It was the correct thing to do.
Everything would turn out right.

Her parents were spending Saturday night with some
friends, so she rang and asked him to come and stay the
night. She met him at the station with the car. In the
garage he kissed her; then he picked her up and carried her
into the house.

Intoxicated by each other's smell and touch and desire,
they started to make love on the floor of the sitting room.
He undressed her slowly, kissing her face, neck, breasts,
and thighs. She pushed him down into the sheepskin rug,
took off his clothes, and made love to him with her mouth.
Then, when he was moaning and tense with want, she
mounted him. After an eternal time of her moving and
weaving and twisting and burning, he came. He held her;
they rested.

When the room grew dark she switched on the lamp
above the mantelpiece. She came and lay beside him. He
made love to her the way she had made love to him before.
She came repeatedly, heaving, gasping excruciatingly into
the quivering warmth of the room above his head. Finally,
like two warm tides merging, they came in unison.

They showered in the upstairs bathroom. Afterwards she

cooked a meal. They ate in silence, completely contained, no need to find each other with words.

Throughout the night, while the dark murmured through the house, they made love in her bed, slept, woke, and repeated the dance of joy as if the morning would see it all end. They were together totally in the present, free of the past and future and even of death; their prisons of flesh and bone and thought transformed into pure emotion, spirit — soaring, wheeling, hovering like the hawk he had once seen holding up the earth on its delicate axis.

After breakfast they went out to the back porch and lay on sun-chairs and gazed up at the gorse-yellow hills. The rose bushes in the garden were covered with dew; in the brittle light they looked like pieces of modern wire sculpture that you could cut your hands on. The glasshouse looked as if it had been carved out of an iceberg. Above everything, the sky was tense, with fists of cloud tinted yellow by the morning light. They could feel the first cold fingers of winter groping into the pores of their skin.

He fell asleep. She got out some fashion magazines and flicked through them. Now and then she glanced over at him and sighed. She would have to tell him that day.

She woke him when it was nearing noon. They had lunch and decided to drive into the city.

The Sunday traffic on the motorway was light. He drove very fast, weaving in and out of the line of cars in front of him. She encouraged him to drive even faster. The car throbbed, purred, pulsated. Like a child enraptured with the freedom of speed, she laughed from time to time. As the car sped towards the city, with the sunlight dancing wildly on the surface of the road ahead and on the sleek steel hides of the oncoming traffic, she shifted over to him and embraced him and flicked her tongue in and out of his ear. She whispered that he was getting her all worked up again. He laughed softly and caressed between her legs. She rubbed herself against his hand and continued to kiss and caress the side of his face.

They parked the car in front of the city railway station and, arm in arm, began walking through the veins of the city. They took the cable car up to the park near the university, sat by the large fountain, and gazed at the city below. They felt as if they owned it all, even the lazy sky stirring contentedly above it. A breathing light seemed to be growing out of the city itself, out of the very buildings that had reminded him of tombs before he had met her. When she remarked that the city was beautiful, he agreed with her.

The paved area round the fountain was soon noisily crowded with the Sunday visitors that the cable car kept bringing up, so they walked back down one of the many winding series of steps so characteristic of the city. At the bottom of the steps, beside the large hotel he usually drank in with his brother and their friends, they stopped in front of the Roman Catholic cathedral.

This impressive building was made of grey stone, mortar, and slate. It was coated with grime and dust, and it seemed to anchor the whole area round it to the ground. It spoke of a permanence that would not change with the city that was constantly changing round it; perhaps of an everlasting guilt, of past errors, now largely forgotten by the city's inhabitants, yet still lodged fitfully in the city's subconscious.

Neither of them had been in the cathedral before. They went up the steps and into the porch. The cathedral was empty. They sat down in a back pew, and he put his arm round her shoulders. She laid her head in the hollow of his neck. Round the bottom of the ornate marble altar, a long line of candles was burning; it threw a trembling current of light over everything near the altar. Above and behind the altar, circling the back wall, huge stained-glass windows blazed hypnotically with all the colours of the rainbow. The rest of the cathedral was still, with a breathless gloom focused on the glittering altar. In turn the altar seemed to suck up their breath to the stained-glass windows, to the central figure of the crucified Christ. For the first time since his childhood he felt he was in a church, part of the mystery that wove the world together in a tapestry of wonder, awe, magic. As he gazed at the

Crucifixion he felt timeless, and capable of believing once again in God.

She began to feel cold. She told him. He got up. She nestled her face into his shoulder and edged him towards the door. He glanced back up over his shoulder at the Crucifixion: the central figure nailed to the Cross seemed outlined by flames; it seemed to detach itself from the window and float slowly towards him.

He looked away quickly and hurried through the door.

For most of the afternoon they wandered aimlessly through the city.

Evening settled down carefully on the city, like a mother bird nestling down over a brood of newly-hatched chicks. They sat on a wooden bench at the edge of a small park in the centre of the city, watching a group of street-corner preachers — two young girls and an elderly man, standing with a microphone on a platform in front of a caravan — conducting a service. On the footpath to the right of the group, were two male guitarists and a woman tambourine player. Some of their congregation were standing on the lawn; some remained in their cars, parked on the road opposite the caravan. The elderly preacher was spitting his frantic sermon into the microphone; the amplified sound burst across the lawn, slamming headlong into the wall of buildings behind the congregation and echoing back.

Tired from walking, they simply listened to the sermon's sound; then the girl lay on the bench with her head in his lap and was soon asleep.

He recognised one of the guitarists, a Samoan he had often seen at the Pacific Islanders church years before when he was a new immigrant. He had looked lost then in his ill-fitting suit. Now he wore a tailor-made suit, a blue tie, a white shirt with a buttoned-down collar, and black shoes polished to snare your reflection in. He exuded an impregnable self-confidence, reinforced by an obviously fervent belief in his brand of fundamentalist religion.

The preacher announced a hymn, the guitarist started to pluck his guitar. There was something about the man he didn't like, so he scrutinised him more closely. Then, as he looked at the other members of the group, he realised what it was. Except for the colour of his skin, the man blended perfectly into the group and was very proud of it: he had become assimilated. He had met Samoans like this man before, and even when he wanted to pity them he despised them. Most papalagi New Zealanders talked of racial integration, but what they wanted was assimilation, the conversion of Polynesians into middle-class papalagi. The process was one of castration, the creation of Uncle Toms.

The girl woke and asked him if the end of the world was at hand yet. They laughed about it.

When the hymn ended, one of the young girls on the platform stepped up to the microphone. She had short black hair that looked luminous in the light of the caravan. She spoke quietly. Her body was resilient and supple, and her voice was gently tinged with a sexual quality. Everyone fell silent.

She was only eighteen, she said. She had left the church three years before and had lived a life of sin. But God had spoken to her during a drug party and she had found the Light again. Modern youth was sick with sin. She knew this because she had lived that sickness: she had committed the grievous sin of fornication with many men, had started drinking and taking drugs. God's love was bigger, more satisfying, than earthly love, she crooned, stroking the stem of the microphone with her hands. She was before all young people to tell them to return to God's mighty love and be saved before it was too late.

The girl beside him laughed behind her hands. She's even got you randy, she whispered in his ear. He broke from the spell. What a waste, she said. Think of all the sinful joy that nymphet preacher could bring you! He told her she was more than adequate for him.

After the service they walked back to the railway station and the car. He opened the car door for her, but she moved into his arms and held him tightly. He asked if anything was wrong.

She told him what she was going to do.

A strange numbness welled up from his lungs to clog his throat, ears, and head, as he watched the car pull away from him. It was as if all sound had been drained out of the city, as if he had suddenly gone deaf. When the car curved round the slow bend in front of the row of billboards by the railway yards, he saw her put her arm out of the window. She waved.

He buttoned his dufflecoat, which smelt of her perfume, turned slowly, and started walking home.

Across from the town hall was a small park made up of two almost leafless trees which seemed to have grown out of the concrete pavement. Under the trees stood two benches. A single street light illuminated the area and the three figures performing a strange dance round the benches. He stopped in front of the town hall and watched.

The figures, clothed in tattered overcoats, were men. One of them was hopping round on one foot, head and shoulders bobbing up and down, while his companions clapped out a slow beat. The dancer reminded him of a pigeon pecking at pieces of bread that someone had scattered on the footpath. Now and again one of the men would stop and drink thirstily from a bottle they were passing round. He remembered that he had once heard someone talking about a place called Pigeon Park which was located somewhere in the heart of the city. Alcoholics and methos gathered there if the night was warm. The dancer stumbled and fell to the ground. Dazed with drink, his friends picked him up, and they all sat down on one of the benches.

He took all the money he had out of his pocket and walked towards them. He could smell the stench of methylated spirits and unwashed bodies even before he reached them, and could hear them mumbling, chuckling, panting, wheezing. They had revived his sense of smell and hearing; the numbness was gone.

Stopping in front of them, his shadow falling over the man in the middle, he suddenly felt he was intruding. The man looked up, his eyes blinking wildly as he tried to stop his heavy head from falling sideways on to his left shoulder. His hair was silver-grey, dry like ash, and his thin face was red and wizened and wrinkled, like the face of a new-born baby. Saliva drooled out of the corners of his toothless mouth. For a tense instant he caught his reflection in the pupils of the man's eyes. He took the man's right hand, turned it palm upwards, placed the money in it, and bent the fingers up round it. The man's hand, now clutching the money securely, dropped down to the bench when he released it.

'Bugger off!' he heard one of the other men mutter.

Turning quickly away from their accusing stare, he started to walk up the street. Where do they find warmth in winter, he thought. The city closed in round him.

She was going to Australia the next week, she had said, gazing into his face. There she would be alone and would be able to think clearly. If she still wanted to have the abortion, she would have it — her father would arrange everything; she would get well and then return to marry him. This would also give him time to make up his mind whether he really wanted to marry her or not. If they got married now, she said, she was positive their marriage would end like her parents' marriage or in a painful divorce. Trust me, she pleaded. She loved him more than anything else. It would be only a short time before she was back. They had to be sure about everything. She would return, they would be married, and there would be nothing between them to ruin their marriage. It was the best way.

I trust you, I love you, was all he could say.

29

She flew to Australia on a wet cold windy Tuesday
morning. He didn't go to the airport to see her off. They
had met the previous afternoon and she had asked him not
to. She didn't want everyone at the airport to see her
crying, she said. They had spent most of the afternoon
sitting on the sea wall at Oriental Bay and talking about
everything else but her going away, until it was time for
her to go home. Then she rushed into his arms and cried.
White-capped green waves were thundering along the
harbour coast and scattering gulls up into the cold air and
overcast sky.

They wrote to each other every day.

She was living in a flat in the middle of Sydney. It
belonged to one of her father's business friends and she
didn't have to pay any rent. She had even been given the
use of a car. She didn't like Sydney, she wrote. It was too
big and impersonal and very lonely. She spent most of her
time watching TV or reading science fiction or writing
letters to him or going to the cinema. Had he seen *Easy
Rider,* she asked. A fantastic film; she had seen it three
times. Every time she got more depressed and missed him
terribly. She urged him to see it. He went, and found it
boring, very pretentious. But he told her that he had
enjoyed it, especially the photography. She wrote back and
compared the journey in *Easy Rider* to their trip round the
North Island. This prompted him to reconsider the film,
and he did see some similarities. He told her this, but said
that Captain America and Billy in the film hadn't found

America, whereas on their North Island trip he had discovered New Zealand. And there hadn't been violent shotgun deaths either. Or marijuana and cocaine. Their trip had been a fantastic love trip not a drug trip to a senseless oblivion of exploding motorbikes. But she had shot that hawk, she wrote back, and he had turned her on with Maui's organ to a rollicking oblivion of exploding nerve-ends. Well, they had got their kicks in the most natural way, he wrote. Captain America and his disciples had been stoned most of the time. He was just a middle-aged young man, that was the trouble with him, she replied. Didn't he realise that the future of the world spoke with an American accent, with Captain America's rather monotonous Yankee twang. Yes, he realised that, he wrote, but what a sad future. In Mao's China, Captain America would be shotgunned as a decadent counter-revolutionary. Billy and Captain America wouldn't be revolutionary guerillas — they couldn't even boil water on an open fire. Che Guevara would be ashamed to have them in his merry band, and Ho Chi Minh, if he was still alive, would definitely not allow them to call him 'Uncle'. Captain America was just another product of upper-middle-class America playing at being a cowboy, and what a sad-faced, middle-aged cowboy he was. Trouble with him, she replied, was that he was too much like that small-town lawyer in the film, all thought and no red corpuscles. Anyway, she admitted, he was right about some aspects of the film. Do you know something? she wrote. I love you, even if you don't like Captain America and Billy and their homosexual motorbikes!

While they had been together in New Zealand he had neglected his studies. Now, to distract his thoughts from her and forget his loneliness and longing, he hurled himself into his work. He attended lectures and seminars in the morning, and spent his afternoons at the National Archives researching his thesis on political development in Western Samoa. After dinner he wrote to her; then, to quell his almost overpowering need to touch her and make love to her and just to hear her, he catalogued the notes he had made that day and worked late on the first draft of his thesis. At the week-end, when he allowed himself to think totally of her, he found himself writing short poems about her and how he felt about her. He sent none of the poems to her; he didn't even mention them. He kept them in the drawer of his desk and reworked them occasionally. After a time he discovered, while rereading some of the poems, that they served to ease his loneliness: they were like friendly companions who talked to him about her. (As literary compositions he was ashamed of them.)

At the end of her second week in Australia she wrote that, after carefully considering the whole matter again, she had decided to go through with the abortion. She had already consulted the doctor who would perform it. Abortions were illegal in Australia but the doctor, a highly respected one, was willing to do it. (He had been hired by her father, she added.) The operation was simple and painless, the doctor had assured her. She would be fully recovered within a fortnight. She missed him, and the longer she postponed the operation the longer she would be away from him. Did he want her to go through with it, she asked at the end of her letter.

He read the letter many times, went for a long walk, returned, and wrote to her. If she wanted the abortion, he said, he feared he might lose her if he tried to stop her. He also believed that the moral implications of the abortion would not disturb her. Like his brother and many others of their generation, she was more a creature of instinct than thought. She lived mainly through the pores of her flesh, through her senses. She was a modern woman; an abortion to her was simply an inconvenience one had to tolerate, a result of forgetting to take the pill one night. And she was doing it for his sake, destroying what she considered was a threat to their happiness in marriage.

In principle he was not against abortion. But in this instance his whole mind and body recoiled from it. The life inside her, lodged in her inner space like a star growing brighter every day and taking on its own identity and beauty and distinctive light and form, was his child, a

157

creation of their love, not a result of a brief meeting of flesh without love. Even though they had not planned to create such a life, it had been created out of love, out of the journey of discovery he had made with her through the North Island which Maui had fished out of the sea's fertile depths. To kill that life would be to distort the meaning of the whole journey and the love they had found for each other.

He didn't tell her this though; he thought she wouldn't understand. He would live with it after they got married; she need never know.

She wrote that he would not hear from her for at least three days. She was to have the operation and then spend a few days in a furnished room near the doctor's clinic, where a qualified nurse would look after her. He worried intensely for four letterless days. When she wrote that the operation had been successful and she was back in her flat, he went drinking with his brother. His brother didn't know what they were celebrating — he didn't tell him. After the pub they went to a friend's home and had an all-night party. It was good to see him back in circulation, his friends said. For a moment there they'd thought he was going to join the unhappy ranks of the ulcerated married.

He slept soundly all day, woke in the evening, and wrote to her, telling her how happy and relieved he was. When was she coming back, he asked.

She didn't reply immediately. This was the first unexplained gap in her letters. He didn't worry about it, but when he received her next letter he trembled as he read it. It was shorter than usual, and, even though it sang with her bubbling vitality, he felt that the joy was slightly contrived. Between the lines, woven unconsciously into the tune of the letter, was an inexplicable note of sadness, faint but still there. She also didn't say when she was returning. In his reply he said nothing of his thoughts. He would wait for her to tell him what was wrong. Her next four letters were of the usual length and type, but she did not mention the abortion nor the date of her return. And the sadness was more obvious. He decided to ask her about it.

There was nothing wrong, she wrote back. At least she couldn't figure out what it was. She only felt that something was just not right. Whenever she was alone — and she was alone most of the time — she felt a depressing longing for something that wasn't there any more. (She wasn't even explaining herself properly, was she, she added.) Whether it was something that had been in her flat, or in her past or present or future, she didn't know. It was so bloody annoying, because she felt she knew what it was, but when she tried to identify it in her mind she just couldn't. She tried to explain it to him another way: it was as if time had stopped for a moment and, when it started again, that moment, that pause, was lost forever, but you continued to feel that it shouldn't have got lost, that it should still be there, because it was vitally important that it should be. You felt cheated but you didn't quite know why and by whom or what. She had started to feel this way when she returned to the flat the third day after the abortion. As soon as she walked through the front door she had felt that the flat was no longer complete, that someone had taken something from it (or something had deliberately got itself lost). She had searched all the rooms. Nothing was missing. She was explaining everything so badly, she said. Was he getting what she meant. Perhaps he could tell her why she felt this way. If she understood what it was, she wouldn't feel so bloody depressed. Apart from this she was fit and healthy and helluva frustrated. (Sexually, she added.) Her heart and soul and centre organ craved for him. She was sure that one luscious Maui stroke and she would be healed, cured, complete again. She went on to say that the doctor was going to examine her for the last time in just over a fortnight. After that she was coming home. Just wait till she got hold of him, she said. He'd die of physical exhaustion!

30

She strolled through the park by the dry shrubs and under the pines, and with a Sunday sun throbbing like a migraine. A circular lake lay in the middle of the park. Over it arched a narrow wooden bridge. She sat down on a bench beside the lake. Three groups of parents and their children were rowing slowly round, tossing pieces of bread to the swarms of ducks and swans. The water made a rapid clapping sound, as the birds, wings beating, fought for the bread. Round the lake shore under the trees other families were having their picnic lunches. As she watched she felt divorced from everything. She bought an ice cream at the crowded park cafeteria and returned to the bench. The ice cream melted quickly in the heat; she licked it a few times and then dropped it into the muddy water. Some ducks were soon tearing it apart in a clatter of wings and stabbing bills.

She gazed into the water. A goldfish flashed for an instant near the surface. Then another one. She thought of him. Then, feeling drowsy from the heat, she stretched out on the bench and went to sleep.

She felt someone tugging at her right hand, and woke up. A little girl with blue-green eyes and long blonde hair and fringe, and dressed in pink shorts and a white blouse with a cartoon of Mickey Mouse on the front, stood gazing down into her face. She sat up. The little girl smiled and said hallo. She asked her if she wanted to sit down. A quick nod and a skip up to the bench. She lifted her on to it.

Ducks, the child said, pointing at the birds floating lazily on the water. And lots of swans too! Looking up at her, the child said that ducks were very good to eat. Some of the ducks quacked from the lake and recaptured the child's full attention; her eyes flashed with utter delight when one of the ducks rose up suddenly and skittered across the water, wings beating down furiously. Then it was free of the water and flying up and around the heads of the trees surrounding the lake. Whe-e-e! the child cried, clapping her hands. Whe-e-e!

She asked the child her name and if someone had brought her to the park. The child pondered for a moment and then divulged her name and said that she had come with her parents and her two brothers and her sister who was only a tiny baby. And where were they, she asked. The child pointed towards the park entrance. She told the child that her mother would probably be looking for her. Still gazing at the ducks, the child said that her best uncle had a farm with lots of ducks on it and geese. And what else? Oh, lots of piggies and horses and lots of puppies who licked her face, and she gave them many loves, and all her uncle's animals loved her and she loved them and she wished she could stay with her uncle all her life and play with the animals. Oh, and her uncle was even getting a big, big giraffe from Africa. She paused, and, looking doubtfully up at the girl, asked if she believed her. She nodded and said that she loved animals too. Her mother and her father didn't believe her, the child said, jumping off the bench.

They went on to the bridge. The child stamped her sandalled feet on the wooden planks and, captivated by the hollow echoing sound, shouted, Nice! Nice! Nice! An old woman who was leaning on the railing turned and smiled at the child. A beautiful child, the old woman said, when she saw her beside the little girl, who had stopped stamping and was now gazing up at the sun as if she was preparing to fly off into it. Is she yours? She hesitated, then nodded her head. Before the old woman could say anything else, she started to steer the child across the bridge. The old woman waved her fingers at the child who turned and waved back.

She bought some peanuts and potato chips and they wandered along the lake shore. The little girl hummed and skipped and stuffed handfuls of peanuts and chips into her mouth. Twice she stopped and scattered chips among the ducks, laughing when they fought for the food.

Once round the lake they sat on the patio in front of the cafeteria and drank cold orange drinks through long thin straws. The child insisted on blowing bubbles into her drink, which annoyed some of the people near them; but she didn't tell her to stop.

Just before they left the cafeteria, the child accidentally spilt the remains of her drink on the table and looked apprehensively at her, expecting to be scolded. She laughed and the child was soon laughing with her. An irate waitress came over and stood above them. The child was frightened of the hefty woman. Some people really spoil their bloody kids, don't they, the waitress said loudly enough for everyone to hear.

She picked the little girl up, and as they walked past the waitress she said, Up you too, butch!

They made their way towards the park entrance, looking for the child's parents. The child stopped and asked her what her name was. She told her. The child repeated it aloud; then, satisfied that she was saying it correctly, reached up and clutched her left hand.

On the lawns under the trees near the main gates were swings, jungle-gyms, and a small merry-go-round. Many children were playing on them. Like an aviary, she thought. The child broke away from her and ran towards the merry-go-round. She started to follow her but stopped when she saw a short chubby woman hurrying out from the shelter of the trees behind the merry-go-round and towards the child. The woman, obviously the child's mother, closed in and cut the child off before she could reach her destination, grabbed her by the shoulder, shook her roughly, and shouted at her. She couldn't hear what the woman was saying. The child burst into tears as her mother pulled her away to where the rest of the family were gathered round a large pram. Just before they reached the others, the woman slapped the child viciously. She couldn't hear the sound of the slap, but she felt the snapping pain in her mind.

She wheeled and fled from the park. The child was gone. Forever. But her presence would continue to haunt her, a ghost she would never be able to exorcise.

31

She wasn't coming back, she wrote to him. She couldn't. She still loved him. Loved him more than ever before. But, if they married, she would destroy him with the guilt, the cold accusing emptiness, she now had to carry. The abortion had been a mistake, a crime, a sin. He should have tried to stop her. She should have done what her heart had wanted her to do, and not have obeyed the cruel objective reasoning of her mind. She had murdered their first child. And it was better for her to live with that, alone. The guilt was hers for the rest of her life. She knew she was hurting him terribly, but he would eventually meet another woman who would be more deserving of his love. Forgive me, she pleaded.

He begged her to return. Together they could learn to forget, and there would be other children. He loved her. Loved her. If she wanted him to, he could come to Australia immediately.

She wrote one more letter to him. She tried to explain. Couldn't. Ended by telling him that she was going to England. She was escaping, but she said she would never really be able to escape because she would always have herself to live with. In England maybe she could forget for a time, she said. Maybe.

The amoral, gay, permissive, fun-loving young are a creation of the mass media, she ended her letter.

32

When the man came through the crowded doorway of the pub he recognised him immediately. The bitter memory of the girl and the party and the man whose party it had been, and of how they had deliberately humiliated him, returned and reopened the pain. Because of her he had allowed himself to be humiliated.

He sipped his beer slowly and watched the man make his way to the bar where he ordered a drink and stood drinking it, his back turned to him. In any group the man would always stand out, with his expensive clothes and his haughty pretensions and manner.

Christmas was only three weeks away. That morning, for three long hours, he had sat his final examination. After having lunch at the student cafeteria he had come to the pub and had got a table on his own. A couple of students he knew vaguely had wanted to join him but he had told them to go drink somewhere else.

He finished his jug of beer, pushed his way up to the bar, and stood beside the man. The barman refilled the empty jug. He glanced at the man beside him. It was him all right: blond, blue-eyed, with an air of smug condescension which reflected the oppressive feel of the city and the people who had taken her away from him. He returned to his table, went on drinking, and waited.

For the first time since he got her last letter he could analyse everything that had happened, with some degree of objectivity. His anger, now controlled like the expert fist of a boxer, was the compass steering him through the maze of self-pity and regret and sorrow and freeing him of them. He focused his total attention on the man at the bar.

Before long the man left the bar and started to make his way through the tangle of people towards the toilets. He got up and followed him. Through the dust-coated window above the door he saw that there was no one else in the toilet. He went in. Locked the door behind him quietly. The man continued urinating into the sheet of water swimming down the wall into the gutter, without turning to see who it was. He stepped on to the raised step in front of the gutter.

'Remember me?' he asked, more to himself than to the man, who began to turn slowly to look at him.

He would never forget the man's amazed expression as the punch exploded at the side of his face, just below his right ear. It was delivered with the brutal force of his weight and strength and anger, the clenched fist crunching into defenceless flesh and bone and surprised fear. The man cried *UHH*!; and his hands automatically clutched at the side of his head as the blow flung him against the wall.

As the man sank down towards the gutter, unconscious, the water washing down from the wall and over his head and shoulders, he hit him just below the heart. 'Now you will always remember me!' he said.

He clutched the lapels of the man's overcoat, pulled him up, and stood him up against the wall. And in a ritual of expert violence he broke the man's ribs with short jabbing punches. (He wasn't going to kill him. He was going to let him live; but the girl, or any other woman, would never again find him a suitable lover.)

Then he worked methodically on his victim's face. (He was only going to break him as a man.)

Then on his victim's manhood.

Afterwards he dragged him into the toilet cubicle and sat him up on the toilet seat, leaning the broken body against the back wall. He came out and shut the door.

He soaked his handkerchief in the sink and used it to wash the blood off his clothes. Then he cleaned his hands, wincing with pain as the water washed over his cut and bruised knuckles.

He suddenly became aware of his reflection in the mirror above the sink. For an unbelievable moment he thought it was someone else, someone he had known well in the past but had forgotten. As he gazed into the face, into the staring eyes, he remembered how, as a child in Samoa, he had watched and then participated in the killing of that boar. It had been a terrifyingly beautiful ritual.

Feeling calm, elated, cool, he returned to his table, drank one more jug of cold beer, and left the pub for the Christmas streets.

That week-end he was returning to Samoa with his parents and brother. For good. Once there he could forget her completely. But, as he walked down the main street of the city, oblivious of the sounds and smells and night colours and the frantic masks of the corridors of steel and plastic, he couldn't hold back the pain. He fled into the shadows of an alleyway and wept. He had received her final letter twenty days before, on a Monday.

She had betrayed him.

But he still loved her. He was sick with the love he felt for her.

PART III

33

The plane landed on the grass runway and moved slowly up to stop in front of the terminal building. He helped his mother with her hand luggage and followed the other passengers to the gangway. (His father and brother had gone on ahead to the terminal building.) The other male passengers — Samoans returning for a vacation — wore charcoal grey suits, dark ties, white shirts, and shiny black shoes; very similar attire to his own. When he noticed this, he wished he had worn something casual so as not to be identified as a New Zealand Samoan. His mother clutched his hand and pulled him through the door.

The moment he emerged from the air-conditioned gloom of the plane, he was blinded by the sun and began to sweat freely. It was as if, like a new-born child, he was being exposed for the first time to the harsh light of day. He stripped off his jacket and draped it across his arm, all the time trying to adjust to the piercing light and heat. His mother tugged at his hand. They moved down the gangway.

Pressed against the mesh-wire fence extending from the terminal building was a crowd of people. Many of them waved and shouted greetings. His mother waved back. He recognised some of his relatives from the photographs which had peopled the walls of their sitting room in New Zealand.

Just before he entered the building, he turned and looked back at the plane. Heat-waves were swimming off it, and it glittered in the light like a large metallic fish which had disgorged him on to the shores of a country real only in myth or fairy tale or dream. Beyond the airstrip, and reminiscent of backdrops in a Technicolor movie of the South Seas, palm trees rolled up to foothills; and beyond them stretched the high volcanic range, greener than anything he had ever seen. It is difficult to die in Samoa, he remembered his father telling him, for Samoa in all its greenness invites you to live. He found himself thinking of the girl, stopped, and went into the building.

When they left the customs area, their relatives and friends swarmed upon them with their incessant warm flowing noise, their utterly open feel and smell and sound, like honey-bees bringing nectar to a nest. His parents and brother opened themselves joyously to the welcome, but he discovered he couldn't, not completely. He watched himself trying to relax, trying to cope with so fervent a welcome from his one remaining uncle, his aunts and their children and their children's children, cousins and more cousins, relatives acquired through history and marriage, and their relatives' friends, and men and their wives and relatives who had known his parents, and many village elders: a world of people he could not hold, embrace, encompass, contemplate, all at once and in that breadth of time. It didn't seem real. They kissed him, strung leis round his neck, fingered his clothes and body, talked to him, all at the same time. Some of the women burst into tears and embraced him again; the men told him they were really proud of him and his accomplishments at university and asked if he was still a great rugby player and boxer. He tried to cope and then edged slowly out of the centre of the group.

At the edge of the circle, however, he was surrounded by a gaggle of children, who pulled at his clothes, giggled, and said his name aloud repeatedly, savouring its novelty. They exuded a strong smell of sweat and coconut oil drying in the heat, the smell of earth after the rain. It thawed to waking the smell of his own childhood. Once he too had been like these children, rich with noise, legs spotted with sores, nose running from daybreak to dusk, the grit and dust of life caught in his fingernails and bare feet, in the grooves of his face, and in his thoughts, a tattered lavalava wrapped round his waist, and with only the promise of adulthood to soothe and bring meaning to the superficial hurts, miseries, disappointments, and tears of a child.

A little boy, head shaven clean of hair, lifted his meagre arms to him. He picked him up and nuzzled his face into the boy's neck. The others sighed and laughed, and all the younger ones clamoured for him to lift them up too. Sweeping two more up with his right arm, he held them against his chest. The three children wriggled self-consciously in his embrace. One of the older children asked him if he could speak Samoan. In silence they waited eagerly for his answer. He rolled his eyes in mock surprise, nodded his head once, twice, three times. They cheered.

When they left the building to go to the bus, which had been hired specially by their relatives to take them to the village about thirty miles away, he noticed that the sun was setting; the whole western horizon seemed to be bleeding. His arms tightened round the children he was carrying.

As the bus creaked over the unsealed road, dancing tiredly over bumps and potholes and ruts, and the darkness closed over the island with a heavy silence, the children he sat with on the back seat fell asleep. Some of the women took them away from him. A few minutes later his brother came and sat down beside him. The others left them alone. Together they watched the villages they were travelling through. Lit by lamps and hemmed in by the dark, the fale were solitary pockets of light guiding them back to the village they had been born in. Occasionally they heard the wailing chorus of cicadas above the roar of the bus.

'It's good to be home, isn't it?' his brother said in English. He remained silent. Only the exhausting move-ment and roar of the bus and the darkness outside had any reality. It was hard to believe that he had spent nearly twenty years preparing and waiting for this return. So many years and now nothing more than an uncomfortable seat, as a stranger, in a bus packed with the mythical characters of the legends his parents had nourished him on for so long.

'Forget her,' he heard his brother say in the darkness. And the reality of New Zealand was with him again.

34

Their first week home was one of feasting. There was a
family feast the night they arrived: roast pork, baked taro,
luau, raw fish, octopus, rock oysters, sea eggs, and many
other foods which they hadn't tasted for nearly twenty
years. Next morning all the village matai came and there
was an ava ceremony of welcome, as was the custom. After
this came another heavy meal and the sharing of food with
all the families in the village. That night, the village
pastors, representing the Methodist, Congregational, and
Catholic churches, came. There was a long evening service
followed by another heavy meal. On Thursday, after family
prayers, the Women's Committee (accompanied by nearly
all the village women) brought gifts of food. Another
sumptuous meal was followed by dancing and singing and
loud laughter late into the night. Friday night brought
nearly all the untitled men, again with gifts of food, and
the ritual of feasting and dancing and singing continued.
Throughout the week, relatives and friends from near and
far arrived with gifts of food. His parents gave all these
groups money or clothes, including clothes belonging to
their sons, and a large suitcase full of candy. On Sunday,
after the morning church service, they had dinner at the
pastor's house with all the village elders.

Early Monday morning he woke to an agonising bout
of diarrhoea, the worst he had ever suffered: almost
constant body-racking vomiting and jabbing stomach
pains, dizziness and cold sweat. His parents went down
with it that night. Only his brother seemed immune. A

woman was sent into Apia hospital for medicine to ease the pain. His parents recovered quickly. He recovered slowly and found he couldn't dispel the disturbing feeling of depression which had set in while he was ill. He tried to recapture the gaiety of the first week but failed. It was as if he had vomited it all out. His mind was analysing the life around him, cutting down through the glittering surface of the myths to the bone. For a few days he tried to stop himself from doing this. Then he gave up; he had to be honest with himself. To deny his thoughts would be to deny a major part of what he was. One had to be honest even with paradise.

He had returned unprepared for the flies and mosquitoes. In New Zealand they had found no place in his parents' stories of Samoa. (Unimportant creatures like these rarely played important roles in any mythology.) Now he had to try to live with them.

Flies seemed to be everywhere, attacking everything — rubbish, food, sores, cuts. In the plantations and bush they were silver-blue monsters, more annoying and braver in their attack. Only when darkness fell did this maddening attack cease. But the dark brought the mosquitoes — a swarming buzzing all round his mosquito net. When they caught him in the open they stung any exposed part of his body. He slapped at them, tried beating them off with a fan. Even safe in his mosquito net he couldn't sleep. He scratched at the spots they had sucked and the spots turned into itchy lumps. A few days later, after more scratching which caused more infection, the red lumps burst into weeping sores.

Then there were all the different sounds which he couldn't adjust to: the incessant throbbing chorus of cicadas at night, which kept him awake: and, when he finally dozed off the sharp squealing of flying foxes, which beat at his eardrums and jerked him awake again; the crashing of the surf, which broke his dreams into irretrievable fragments; before dawn the snorting rage of pigs and the piercing crowing of roosters; and throughout the night the hungry barking of dogs.

During the day he couldn't escape the noise and smell of people. They were all round him, enveloping him in their chatter, laughter, crying, arguing, growing, movement, especially the children. He tried at times to catch the silent pauses, but just when he thought he had snared them someone would shatter them, take them away from him. He longed to hear the sounds of the city again. (At least he was used to them.)

Then there were the great silences which fell at evening just before the sun toppled into the sea, and immediately before and after evening prayers. He heard these silences clearly when they were born out of the sun's dying. He was afraid of them because they exposed him utterly to his own fears, to the clarity of his mind, and finally to that silence when the flesh ceases to breathe. In a city he could escape them. Here he had to confront them, and with them the terror that they unleashed inside him. And always the girl occupied his mind with the silences, growing in the dark.

When he was sick with diarrhoea, he suffered the humiliation of the family outhouse often. Though dazed with illness, he still couldn't ignore the stench of human excrement and the swarm of flies that went with it in the daytime. And there was no toilet paper. The outhouse was situated under a stand of breadfruit trees behind the group of family fale. He felt that everyone was watching him go to it. For him, the path to it was paved with humiliating embarrassment. Every time he imagined the whole family joking among themselves about him, the very palagi son. A group of children usually followed him. They waited outside for him, and when he took too long they rapped on the door, which was full of holes and cracks, or peered at him. He ordered his mother to order the children not to follow him. She did so; but the children, who admired him as their new hero, took no notice. When he recovered he laughed when they asked him to describe what toilets were like in New Zealand. Was it true that palagi people had their toilets inside their houses next to their bedrooms and where they ate? And where did they store the stuff, one boy asked politely.

He was also upset by the rudimentary standards of sanitation and hygiene in the village. There was a small hospital at the northern end of the bay, but only serious cases were taken to it. Very critically ill patients had to be sent to the hospital in Apia. But for almost every malady the remedy was massage, and only when lengthy, often agonising, periods of this treatment failed was the patient referred to a doctor. Most of the children were spotted with sores; little was done to help them to heal. It was taken for granted that leaving them open to the elements was the best cure. Some of the children suffered from malnutrition, but to point this out to their parents was considered an insult — no one in Samoa suffered from malnutrition! Many children looked under-nourished, there were serious imbalances in their diet. He was shocked by the condition of the few people who had filiariasis — bloated legs and arms spotted with ugly sores. There was little tuberculosis and leprosy, and he was thankful for that. Few rules of cleanliness were observed in preparing food, but he had to admit that only papalagi and very papalagi Samoans like himself got ill from eating the food. 'Samoan stomach', papalagi called it. It should be called 'papalagi stomach', he thought. He also had to admit that, despite the visible effects of the ravages of disease, the people, especially the men, were physically the most beautiful he had seen. They reminded him of figures in Greek sculpture — at least before middle-age and the quick sag into flab and fat.

Further observation and analysis would lead him to more penetrating conclusions, and he would have to agree with much of what his father had told him in New Zealand, and to disagree with much of what his mother had said.

His people — and it was difficult for him to refer to them as his people because he was now more papalagi than Samoan — measured life in proportion to their physical beauty, gauging a man's courage by what they so aptly called his 'gut-content'. To survive, he concluded, a male had to rise to any insult or ear-pulling with silent and fearless fists; settle any argument, when verbal virtuosity proved inadequate, with flailing hands. And it didn't matter whether one was five years old or burdened with wrinkled old age. This led him to conclude further that his people lived primarily through the flesh, priding themselves on the flexibility of their muscles, glorifying physical courage and unmaimed flesh. That was why, he noticed, the main targets for their jokes and ridicule were people and animals with physical or mental defects: hunchbacks, the blind, albinos, the mentally handicapped, the limbless, the crippled, the mute and deaf, the insane. Considering themselves perfect physical specimens, they frowned upon training for any kind of sport. They believed themselves innately fit: one was born fit, and fitness remained with one until one died. He noticed in relation to this that they measured themselves in terms of how much punishment and pleasure the flesh could consume and endure. Quantity of consumption was the measure. So every feast was an orgy of food. The cultivation of jowls, paunches, flab, and short-windedness seemed a national hobby; they seemed to invite obesity, diabetes, and heart-attacks. Yet he sensed that they were secretly ashamed of their gluttony for things of the flesh. But why feel ashamed, he thought. It was a sign of spiritual and emotional health that they hadn't yet stopped living through the flesh; that, unlike Westerners (and Samoans like himself), they hadn't learnt to spurn things of the flesh; that good living was eating, drinking, laughing, screaming, weeping, fucking, dying: an orchestra of emotions transmitted through the flesh, communicated through the pores; knowing but not really caring that the flesh was mortal. His people lived in the present and it was good. (He knew he couldn't; not any more.) Related to this, even the violence they heaped on one another seemed all in the present. Their tempers would explode and they would send one another to hospital with stone or machete or fist wounds. Then deep remorse, and all was forgiven. To them there was no such creature as an irredeemable sinner. Rarely did they premeditate violence. Premeditation supposed a mind that lived and planned for the future. And rarely did they commit violence for personal gain.

Murder was usually to right an insult to one's family. And one's family was all-important. Loyalty to the family came before everything else, even one's life.

Their pretensions, he concluded, like their exaggerated faith in their physical courage, were of gigantic proportions. Samoa was the navel of the universe: the world ended within the visible horizons and reefs. Anything beyond that was impossible tales of pagans and gangsters and cowboys, and unreasonable wars fought between Communists and Americans. What was real were their islands — magnified in their hearts into an emotional and spiritual heaven larger than the planet itself. Totally committed to the present, Samoa was the present, and the sacred centre of the universe. Related to this, they maintained that they were the only true Polynesians left in the world. More important still, they were Samoan, and by this very fact superior to all other human beings. As he analysed village and national politics, he had to conclude that his people aspired to titles more aspiringly, as it were, than all other pursuers of titles. None of them were commoners: they were all descendants of nobles — noble 'noble savages', noble nobles. And because of this there was equality. In public they feigned humility, until they were challenged (or felt challenged) to reveal their blue-bloodedness; then humility was shattered and, enraged, they recited the litany of genealogical trees higher than other noble trees in the nobility forest. Everybody was a somebody, and individual identity was lost in a pantheon of gods. The acquisition of titles, whether real or imaginary, was an endless battle, a dynamic force in village life.

After a few months of listening and observing, he concluded that their respect for the spoken word was equal to their respect for physical courage. In the villages, the orators were the people with real political power and influence. They were the poets, the song-makers, the historians, the politicians, the peacemakers (and the destroyers of peace). Many of them were barely literate; yet to listen to them — to their weaving of a tapestry of image, sound, meaning, and emotion — was to listen to gifted artists performing on a many-stringed instrument; was to hear the true power of poetry with the breaking open of the rich seeds of the spoken word. Many of the orators were wonderful liars and confidence men, but it was expected of them. They had to live by their wits, take on the best orators in the other villages and, in a stunning battle of verbal wizardry, win for their village and district. If they suffered defeat their village suffered that defeat too. A defeated orator was a prophet without honour, a disgrace to his district. Victory was not confined to emotional rewards: there were fine mats, food, money, and political power to be won. As his uncle explained to him, a great orator could wring music, laughter, anger, and joy out of a dry stone, and make you believe anything. Great orators, his uncle claimed, possessed the magic of the word and therefore the true power of thought and feeling. A man who had the gift of words was truly inspired; he was human yet he possessed the essence of immortality because only the word was eternal. The word separated man from the beast, his uncle said. Sons of men were fed on words. Therefore a human being had to learn to respect the magic of language and those fortunate people who had the gift. Respect for the correct use of language, his uncle said, was peace, harmony, civilisation. To say, like many arrogant papalagi, that Samoans had no language worth considering was to say that Samoa had no culture, that Samoans were only slightly removed from the beast.

One of the most vital features of village life that he would never be able to compromise with, he found, was the power of the pastors and the church and the religiosity of the people, even when he realised that Christianity had been changed in the image of the fa'a-Samoa, the Samoan way of life; and that to destroy it would be to undermine the fa'a-Samoa, to root out of his people's minds a living part of themselves. Religion was a social custom, a major strand in the social, economic, and political web. God, so his uncle declared, was in the food they ate, in the water they drank, in the air they breathed, in the earth they trod on and died on, in the words they spoke, in the sleep they slept and the dreams they dreamt, in the Everywhere and Everything. He wanted to laugh, but stopped himself when he sensed that his uncle was serious.

Because he didn't want to hurt his own family by exposing them to village criticism, he agreed to accompany his parents and brother to church on their first Sunday home. But he adamantly refused to wear his charcoal grey woollen suit and the tie and shoes his mother wanted him to wear. His mother longed to impress the village. But he wasn't a palagi showpiece or a sophisticated New Zealand Samoan, he muttered to her. He borrowed a white lavalava from one of his cousins, put on a white shirt, and went barefooted.

As soon as they entered the packed church, he ducked away from his mother and sat down beside some youths in the back pew. The rest of his family continued up the centre aisle. Everyone watched them. He felt ill with embarrassment. His mother strutted in her most expensive suit, hat, and earrings, with shiny red lipstick and a heavy handbag, as if she was sole owner of the universe. His father walked with bowed head, as if he was looking for a hole in the solid concrete floor to hide in. His brother — immaculate and condescendingly handsome in his Italian-style suit, bell-bottom trousers, tan shoes polished to ensnare any naive woman in, red silk handkerchief poking out of his front suit pocket like a flower, long hair, and sideboards slick with hair-oil — was out to win the girls. His parents and his brother sat down in the pew directly in front of the pulpit. The service started and almost everyone concentrated on observing them.

Gradually, as the service progressed, he relaxed and found himself enjoying it, especially the singing. But, when the pastor (who, he concluded, was a rotund caricature of the typical pastor he had heard about) got up to preach, he wanted to escape from the clinging heat of the church.

The pastor was obviously addressing his sermon to the exiles who had returned from New Zealand and ignoring the rest of the congregation. He peppered his sermon — a pompously loud, bubbling brew of platitudes, homilies, arrogance, and threats — with English words and expressions, which he then translated hurriedly into Samoan for the benefit of the less educated.

That afternoon, after the two-hour exhausting dinner at the pastor's house and a short fitful sleep, he woke to the clanging church bell and tried to sneak out of the fale, but his mother caught him. So he had to attend the afternoon service. This time his mother made sure he sat with her in the front pew. After all, he was the best-educated son of the village and of Samoa, and the ordinary people had a right to see and admire him, she told him. If they found out that he was an atheist (and it was difficult for her even to utter this horrible word) they might as well return to New Zealand. There was no place in Samoa for atheists. Just pretend, she pleaded with him.

When the last hymn ended, two deacons went up and sat at the table below the pulpit. He knew immediately what was going to happen. He got up to leave, but his mother clutched the side of his lavalava and forced him to sit down.

One of the deacons began to call out the names of each family. With a grand flourish his mother clicked open her fat handbag and started to count the wad of money she had in it. He bowed his head. Representatives from each family were going up to the deacons to give their donations. Each donation was recorded in an exercise book and the amount read out to the congregation. As yet no family had given more than ten dollars.

Their family's name was called. A deep expectant silence fell on the church. His mother held the thick wad of notes towards him. He refused to take it. He even refused to look at her. Angry, but smiling all the while, she thrust it into his brother's eager hands. His brother rose, the splendour of his attire and smile dazzling all the women, and with long military strides marched up to the deacons, laid the money in front of them for everyone to sigh about, wheeled, smiled at the congregation, and floated back to his seat.

A hundred dollars! the tall, lean, hungry-looking deacon announced. The congregation sighed in wondering amazement. The pastor beamed in his pulpit.

With this powerful display of wealth, which was in total accord with customary practice, his family had become accepted as a wealthy and God-loving unit of the village. The move was convincing proof of true aristocratic breeding, high status, and godliness. All genuine wealth should be displayed openly and shared with the church and everyone else. One's alofa for God, family, village, and country had to be proved constantly. Such proof was shown in loyal service, donations of money, pigs, fine mats, and anything else the loved one expected. To say that one had genuine alofa for God, family, and so forth was not genuine alofa. One had to give visual proof, and the quality of one's alofa was evaluated in terms of the quality and quantity of this proof. Tears, sobs, laughter, words, silent respect and obedience, wordy repentance, could be offered as proof, but the quality of the alofa still depended on the quantity of the visual proof. A hundred dollars was real quality alofa, he thought.

In the following months he made further observations about religion, and he had to agree with a lot of his mother's claims after allowing for her exaggerations. One afternoon he made the mistake of telling her this. She spent the next hour re-explaining them. When she reiterated that God had given them the fa'a-Samoa and only He could take it away, he unwisely reminded her that the fa'a-Samoa had been in Samoa a long time before Jehovah was brought to the islands. Wisdom gave way to controlled anger and she told him that the trouble with the modern generation was that they had no faith in their elders' wisdom; that modern youth were simply long-haired, godless, over-educated fools who were turning into decadent papalagi. He said that he didn't want to argue with her, that he respected his elders as a good Samoan child should; and he got up and left the fale to go swimming in the afternoon sea.

One observation which he made later, was that most of his people had implicit (or was it explicit?) faith in the Bible, the Book. Religious, political, and intellectual debates started with the Book. Cornered in a religiously religious argument, an opponent would say, 'But it's in the Book!' And with this magic charm he would avert defeat by forcing his opponent into a very hazardous position: to challenge or question the Book's authority was an heretical act; to say that the Book was wrong was to invite God's fearful wrath.

He found too that his people tended to interpret the Book literally. Adam and Eve had been live people, the Snake had been a slippery snake, and the apple they had so foolishly eaten was an apple very similar to the apples which were imported from overseas (and which only a few of them had ever tasted). Hell was a stormy sea of liquid fire in which the Damned would continue to swim, groan, and gnash their sharp teeth until Judgement Day, when God would separate the sheep from the goats. Heaven, on the other hand, was a utopian colony of milk and honey wherein the Blessed sat at God's feet and hymned hymns all eternity long. God had created the heavens and earth in six days; on the seventh day he had rested. Darwin was an evil liar, the Devil had led him to evolution and the ape. Any sane human being only needed to see his reflection to know that he looked nothing like an ape!

The Book was also poetry, and their main source of reading. Every family had more than one Bible. There were few other books in their homes. At night and on Sunday he spent pleasant hours listening to the old people reading aloud from Psalms or Ecclesiastes, his favourite books of the Bible. They made the words, the music, and the images come alive like beautiful birds hovering in a clear windless sky, or multicoloured fish darting in and out of the fabulous coral of the reefs. Like poets, they believed fervently in what they were reading. During these moments of peace, the memory of the girl did not cause him pain and he was free of self-pity and regret.

35

He discovered the stone grave accidentally, stumbling over
it on to his knees as he wandered through one of the ancient
palm groves in the family plantation. It was buried under
a thick smother of creepers, weeds, and shrubs. At first,
after he had groped through the creepers with his hands
and found the three stone tiers, he didn't think of clearing
it. He gazed up at the murmuring heads of the palm trees
that stood round him in a circle. The shimmering light of
the late morning sun, radiating from the green leaves and
fruit, numbed his eyes for a moment. He remembered that
his grandfather was buried in one of the groves. He started
weeding the grave.

It took him nearly an hour. He did not pause; he worked
as though he was trying to uncover an important mystery
which lay buried within himself. His tender hands ached,
the insides of his fingers were covered with ugly stinging
blisters, and his clothes were drenched with sweat by the
time he finished. But he felt cool, with a secure sense of
elation, harmony. In New Zealand his father had avoided
talking to him about his grandfather; and he had never
asked about him, sensing that it would cause his father too
much pain.

Free of tenacious creeper and weed, the grave dried
quickly in the sun; the dark wet stones took on the colour
of grey ash while he watched from the shade of a palm tree.
Lying in the centre of the grove, the grave gave the circle
of palms a feeling of completion; the centre, the axle of the
wheel, was still there. Mosquitoes and flies buzzed round

him but they didn't bother him — he had rubbed insect repellent into his skin before venturing into the plantation.

He imagined that his grandfather had been extremely independent, an eccentric loner who treasured solitude. At least, in the few months since their return to Samoa, that was what the old people had told him. From their guarded conversations about his grandfather he had concluded that nearly everyone had been afraid of him, of what one toothless old man called his grandfather's 'love of the darkness', and of his haughty disrespect for anyone who felt secure only in a group, a mob, a tribe, a community. One night, alone with his uncle after everyone else had gone to sleep, he asked him about his grandfather. Even his uncle was afraid: he evaded the question by saying that his grandfather had been 'a good Christian'. Was it true grandfather was insane, he asked next. His uncle blinked, shuddered, and in a shocked voice asked who told him that. No one, he said, shrugging; he had heard it somewhere. His uncle got up and went to bed. After that no one in the family divulged to him any detailed, honest information about his grandfather. Not even his usually talkative mother.

As he sat in the shade, and the sun burnt a track in the sky towards noon, he sifted the information he had gathered and, combining it with what he knew of his father and family, began to plait it into an image, a man, whom he then fitted into the history of the village and district. His imagination breathed life into the image and gave birth to an epic myth, an imaginary companion to keep him strong in his loneliness and his quest for solitude. A long lizard, the colour of midnight, started to slide out from one of the gaps between the stones, saw him, and darted out of its lair. He watched it wriggle into the safety of the creepers encircling the grave. A tremor of fear jabbed through his tongue, like an almost painless needle, when he remembered that the black lizard had been believed to be a manifestation of one of the gods in pre-Christian Samoa. The loud silence of the greenery around him pulsated in his ears. But he didn't flee from the palm grove back to the village where the unceasing noise of people would distract him from the penetrating gaze of his own fears. He concentrated on recapturing the man he had resurrected, refashioned, created. And when this being, with whom he now felt an inseparable affinity, was whole again, his fear was gone, exorcised by his grandfather's warm magic.

His grandfather was born in the second half of the nineteenth century; too early to become a tame part of the world that the papalagi were establishing in Samoa, and too late to become an obedient member of pre-papalagi society. He was born two months prematurely, during an eclipse of the sun. (Both were omens of greatness, the old people predicted.) He was also born the youngest son of a notorious war priest who had been killed in a brutal battle fifty days earlier.

An autocratic tyrant, his grandfather's father had pursued military glory, honour, and a reputation as a warlord genius, with a tenacity and ferocity which even a white shark couldn't match. He lost an eye (the right one), sold much of the district's lands to buy muskets, cannon, dynamite, and ammunition, fed three of his sons into war's gluttonous gob, and then in his last battle lost his nerve — the missionaries were at the time tempting him with hypnotic visions of possessing a greater kingdom and eternal life — and was chopped into little bloody pieces by his enemies, using the new steel axes.

Before his grandfather was born, his father had predicted for him the life of a conqueror in the kingdom the missionaries were forging: he was to be a Christian so that he could gain the secret of Jehovah's mysterious powers and use it to enslave all Samoa. The fulfilment of that prophecy never even got off the ground, as it were. A month after his grandfather was born, a whimpering weak clot of blood, so the old people said, his mother (whom the missionaries found easy to convert after the warriors brought home her husband's scattered remains) died from a broken heart, made more broken on seeing the ugly clot of blood she had given birth to.

His grandfather's grandmother, famous throughout the islands for her healing skills and supernatural powers, got a young mother to feed the baby. She also nursed him, sang, and turned him with her delicate hands into the handsomest devil in the district. (The clot grew into an irresistible cock, he would boast when he was an old man.) His poor misguided father had wanted him to conquer through the palagi musket, but he grew to conquer through his healing powers and what came to be known as his 'epic phallus'.

She trained him to use all the traditional cures, and he proved exceptionally gifted. She also educated him in those cures that were peculiarly her own: silence, solitude, courage; a detailed knowledge of history, oratory, warfare, legends and myths, biology, the stars and how to read them, the sea and how to respect it and live harmoniously with it; how to resist the nubile wiles of Jehovah; how to interpret signs and omens; how to appease the gods, to bribe, to tame them; how to cure, conquer, tame, and release any shade of woman. And how not to be afraid of anyone, dead or alive, or of himself.

Because everyone, including the missionary pastors, was terrified of her, no one dared to interfere with the very full education she gave him.

When he grew to manhood he revelled with arrogant delight in his conquest of the female members of all the families who had turned Christian. She travelled far and wide, invited by people to heal the sick, exorcise ghosts, predict the future, ease the agony of giving birth and dying, interpret dreams, perform miracles (and expose miracles performed by others). He accompanied her everywhere she went. That everywhere always led to many broken maidenheads (belonging to young or well-chaperoned and well-guarded maidens) and broken hearts (belonging to women who had lost guard and chaperon uncountable times somewhere along their line of growing up). Enraged fathers and mothers (and their enraged families), enraged husbands (and their enraged families), enraged missionaries (and their enraged pastors) rarely dared to try to oppose him. They were all afraid of his mysterious powers (and even more afraid of his grandmother).

He was nearly thirty-five years old when she died; he had never taken any one woman to be his permanent wife according to Christian practice. By this time his reputation as a healer, and the people's fear of him, were well-established.

He oiled his grandmother's body with coconut oil, wrapped it in tapa cloth and fine mats, wound layers of sinnet round it, and in the middle of the night took her out well beyond the reef in a canoe, tied the canoe anchor round her feet and eased her down into the sea's cold vault. He returned home and disappeared into the mountains for forty days and forty nights.

His grandmother died a pagan, leaving him a feared oddity in a tame ocean full of nominal Christian fish, eagerly pursuing the 'Light' but haunted by wrathful ghosts, insatiable gods who ruled the unfigleafed phallus, and by guilty memories of freedom and grace before the Fall — white sailing ships bursting out of the sky with their voices of phosphorescent fear.

A year after his grandmother's death he took a wife. They even married in church. There was great rejoicing in the village. Now he was one of them; they need not be afraid of him any more.

A cool breeze wove lazily through the grove, whispering, playing with the foliage. He emerged breathlessly from the refreshing pool of his thoughts. The stones of the grave were brittle dry. Around it the piles of uprooted creepers and weeds that he had made hummed with insects. Giant ants trailed in and out of the gaps between the stones. The air smelt of crushed leaves and drying mud. It was time for the midday meal, and if he wasn't there they would come to look for him.

As he strolled back through the plantation, he reflected that his family — through no deliberate plan or wish — had inherited from history a mammoth skeleton which they had so far been able to imprison safely in the family cupboard (throwing away the key by never talking about the skeleton even in a whisper). But that skeleton was too epic (or was the appropriate adjective 'notorious') to wish away into the realm where all other nightmare ghosts were reshaped as harmless or heroic characters in pleasant fairy tales. For his family, grandfather was too titanic a nightmare to turn into an honourable figure in the family's pantheon of gods: darkness clung to him; he stank too much of the time before the coming of the Light.

He felt like dancing, singing. However, as he broke from the shade of the gnarled cacao trees and started to clamber up the high rock fence behind his family's kitchen fale, a question choked back his feeling of joy: why had his grandfather married, and in church, and to that particular woman. And why, in all that he had heard of his grandfather, was there no mention of her.

He wished he had not resurrected his grandfather, given flesh and soul and breath to the skeleton, for his creation was beginning to haunt him too. And now there was another woman also, his grandmother.

That night, while he lay in the darkness under his mosquito net, he found himself thinking of her: she had the face, the voice, the feel of the girl he had lost in New Zealand. Sweeping aside the net, he groped his way out of the fale. Now the two women were one; he couldn't escape. He knew why his grandfather had married and how his grandfather's life had ended. He tried to understand as he stood on the beach and the waves sucked at his feet and filled the dark with their muted sobbing.

For the first time since their return, he wanted to get away from the village altogether. At least for a few days. Away even from his parents and brother.

His father and a gang of carpenters were finishing their new house. It had four bedrooms, a large sitting room, a flush toilet, a dining room and a kitchen, all screened against insects and proofed against termites. Two large concrete tanks would feed water into the house. There was to be electricity too, supplied by a small generator. A small store was to be built in front of the house near the road to sell essential foodstuffs and frozen meat and fish.

His brother had bought a new bus and ran it daily between the village and the town; he was planning to buy two more. He was already an admired, dynamic, generous member of the group of untitled men in the village. All the mothers were competing (not too openly though) to marry their daughters to him.

His mother was now a pillar of the Women's Committee: a generous, conscientious member who was aspiring to capture the leadership of the committee before long. She was very active in all church affairs and was the first woman to be elected to the village school committee. She was envied by all the other women for her spectacular clothes and shoes and her cosmetics.

His parents and his brother were achieving permanence in the village and thoroughly enjoying it. Inevitably therefore a gap was opening between him and them, for he was suffering from a dreaded feeling of unreality. The village seemed unreal and impermanent. He couldn't persuade himself that he could live and marry and die in it. He wanted to, but he knew he couldn't, and hated himself for knowing it. Associated with this knowledge was a mounting sense of guilt: if he left he would be betraying his parents and the twenty years they had spent in exile so that he could get a good education. Perhaps he could live in Apia, he thought.

As he walked back to bed he decided to visit the town for the first time. (He had avoided it since their return.) Stay in a hotel. Escape Samoa for a while. Enjoy a period of complete privacy and solitude — things he treasured but hadn't found in the village in eight months.

36

The bus stopped at the new town market. All the other passengers got off. He asked his brother to take him out to the hotel, which was only a short distance away. Puzzled, his brother looked at him. He repeated his request. His brother drove him to the hotel.

His brother asked him if he needed any money. He shook his head and said that he was going to stay in Apia for a few days. Anticipating his brother's next question, he added that nothing was wrong; he only wanted to be away from the village for a while, to see the town. Need any money? his brother asked again. He didn't answer. Taking out his wallet, his brother sheathed it in his shirt pocket, pushed him gently out of the bus, told him to have a good time, and drove off.

As he watched the bus turn on to the main street, he remembered that he hadn't told his parents what he was going to do. He was glad he hadn't — he wanted to be left alone completely. He went into the hotel lobby.

He had read somewhere that the hotel was one of the oldest buildings in the country. It had been built at the end of the nineteenth century by a German trading firm. It was also the largest wooden building in Samoa. The week before he had read in the local newspaper that the hotel was to be pulled down. A new tourist hotel was to be built on the site.

There was no one in the lobby. Just a long open bar at the far side, a collection of varnished wooden chairs and tables, and a tapa-cloth mural on the wall. The late morning sun was streaming through the large windows round the immense room. Flies were weaving in and out through the streams of light, like tiny leaves caught in the currents of a lazy river. The wooden floor was shiny black with age. A cat peeped out from underneath the bar and then withdrew out of sight.

He walked up to the receptionist's desk with his small suitcase in which he had packed some clothes, a toothbrush, toothpaste, and a comb. He shook the small handbell timidly. The tinkling sound trembled in the still emptiness of the lobby for an instant. He waited. No one came. He rang again. A door slammed somewhere down the corridor to his left. Footsteps started thudding towards the lobby. He turned and faced the open door.

A girl came through the doorway, yawning and brushing her hair down with her hands. She wore pink lipstick, long earrings, numerous bangles round her left wrist, a silver watch, high-heeled shoes, and an extremely short mini, which showed her thick thighs and clung tightly round her body; her abundant breasts were thrust out provocatively. She saw him, smiled, scrutinised him — he was wearing a lavalava and T-shirt and was barefoot — stopped smiling, came to the desk, sat down, took out an account book, and started to check it as if he wasn't there.

'Do you have any rooms?' he asked in Samoan.

'Who for?' she asked in English, without looking up at him, her fingers drumming on the account book.

Trying not to get angry and pretending that he didn't understand English, he said, 'May I have a room, please.'

She snapped the account book shut, and in a mixture of English and Samoan said, 'Do you have any money to pay for it?'

He took the wallet out of his shirt pocket, opened it while she watched him, and thrust it close to her nose.

She straightened up when she saw the money. 'How long are you going to stay?' Again the mixture of English and Samoan.

He shut his wallet and put it back in his pocket. 'Don't know yet.'

She looked at his suitcase. 'It isn't often we get *Samoans* staying here,' she said. He concluded that, when she spoke Samoan, she couldn't help using English with it.

'And aren't you a Samoan?' he asked. She looked puzzled and hurt, so he said, 'Just give me a room.'

She took him upstairs and showed him a small dingy room. He walked down the corridor, found a larger room which overlooked the front lawns and the sea, went in, put his suitcase on the bed, and told her he was going to have that room. Before she could protest, he steered her out of the room and shut the door in her face.

'Bloody Samoan!' he heard her say in English as she went away.

He hadn't had a hot shower since he left New Zealand. He took one, and stood under the warm current for nearly an hour, loving it, the pores of his body and mind opening like petals to drink in the soothing heat. Then he dried himself, locked the doors of his room, lay down naked on his bed, and toppled into deep sleep — the most refreshingly complete sleep he had had since his return. He dreamt of burning sun on snow, of the cold winds that blow in from the Pole, of fairy-tale sheep, light as feathers, gambolling across hills lush with grass, greener than the waters within a reef. He dreamt he was the clouds massing, weaving themselves into all the shapes imaginable, stretching out to heal the past, the present, the future by fusing all into one horizon, one being.

The fierce clanging of a gong woke him. His belly groaned with hunger. He went in search of the dining room. There were about ten people in the room, all tourists. They all looked alike — middle-aged, tired, faces peeling with sunburn, all trying frantically to enjoy the expensive holiday they had spent many years saving up for. He took a table in the far corner, away from them. He waited. He watched them.

No one came to serve him. The two waitresses, who were hovering efficiently round the other guests, seemed to be avoiding his table. Noticing the way they kept looking at him, he realised that they were puzzled, amused, offended almost, by his presence in the hotel. He motioned to one of them to come over. She came reluctantly, as though she didn't want anyone, especially the tourists, to see her obeying him.

'I'd like something to eat,' he said to her in Samoan. She glanced back at the other waitress and shrugged her shoulders and rolled her eyes, as if to indicate that he was slightly insane. 'I'm staying here and I can afford to pay,' he added.

'I'll have to check on that,' she said. (Like the receptionist, she spoke in a mixture of English and Samoan.) She wheeled to go.

'Look, my bloody money is the same as any palagi's or half-caste's,' he said in English. The fact that he could speak English (and English of high quality) did the trick. It proved to her that he wasn't trying to have a free meal, that he wasn't a Samoan from what the townsfolk referred to cynically as 'the back districts'.

She served him lunch.

For the rest of his stay in the hotel and in Apia he had no more trouble. He used English or the unique town mixture of English and Samoan whenever he wanted something. He didn't really like doing this, but because he wanted peace of mind he did it. Money and the quality of a person's English were two of the town's peculiar ways of estimating status. To be fluent in English and yet speak to someone in Samoan was interpreted by that someone as an insult, a deliberate attempt on your part to show that the unfortunate someone didn't know any English. Good English was proof that one was educated, sophisticated, civilised, totally removed from an 'uneducated villager from the back'.

After lunch he wandered through the town. When he came to the public library he went in.

He moved from bookshelf to bookshelf, choosing books at random, flicking through them, savouring their rich feel and aroma: a world he had missed for nearly ten months. He felt alive, his pulse spinning giddily with happiness. He stayed until a librarian told him that they were closing for the day. The next morning he was the first person to enter the library. He paid his subscription, chose a stack of novels, journals, magazines, and newspapers and rushed back to the hotel.

On the veranda outside his room there was a cane sofa. He stretched out on it and, in the cool breeze from the harbour, read avidly until noon when, to his surprise, the waitress who had served him the day before came and told him that lunch was nearly over.

He felt ravenously hungry and he gorged himself. Nothing else in the room existed but food. The waitress refilled his plate as soon as he emptied it. An hour later he finished, realised what he had done, and apologised to her. She laughed and told him not to worry about it. He left a large tip on the table and went back to his room and another healing bout of sleep. He woke in the evening. The money he had given her was on his bedside table.

He didn't go in to dinner. He read until dawn.

He woke before noon, showered quickly, hurried back to the library, returned the books he had borrowed, and got another stack. When the waitress knocked on his door and asked him if he wanted any lunch, he said no. Was everything all right, she called. He didn't even hear her. She waited for a minute longer outside the door and then left.

When the room grew unbearably hot, he put on a lavalava and shifted out to the veranda and the cane sofa. Just before the library closed for the day he went and borrowed some more books.

The lobby and bar were crowded when he returned. He sat at one of the vacant tables reserved for guests and, while skimming through the stack of books, drank cold beer after cold beer. He didn't even notice how much he was drinking. It had no effect on him.

Someone sat down in the chair opposite him. He smelt perfume and looked up. It was the receptionist. He went on reading.

'Hey!' she said. 'Do you always read that much?' He pretended he hadn't heard her. She leant forward and tapped him on the shoulder. 'Boy, you're a real reader, aren't you!'

He shut the book and asked her if she wanted something to drink.

'Seeing I'm off work now, okay,' she said. She called one of the waiters and ordered a bacardi and coke. 'And the most educated Samoan on the island is paying for it,' she told the waiter.

'Who are you referring to?' he asked.

'Boy, you're really slow for someone with two university degrees!' she replied. Unfolding a newspaper, she showed him an article about himself. He looked at it briefly, cursing his parents (or had it been his brother?) for putting it into the newspaper. 'And every local in the hotel is talking about you. We didn't know we had such a hero in our midst.' He pushed the newspaper back across the table to her. 'Aren't you interested in reading about yourself?'

'Not very much,' he replied, sipping his beer and gazing at her. From the beginning of his stay she had treated him with arrogant disdain. Now it was different. His degrees gave him meaning for her, the beauty of the civilised villager, the next best thing to a papalagi. Her classification of him was so correct, he thought bitterly. And she could only accept him as that.

They drank and talked. She did most of the talking. She had been to a good school, she said. She had her School Certificate but had failed to get a government scholarship to go to New Zealand. All her life she had wanted to go to business college in New Zealand. She had many relatives there. She wanted to get away from this small country, to be free of its ignorance. She asked him to tell her about New Zealand. He distracted her by asking if she wanted another drink.

She rambled on: endless chatter about the latest fashions in shoes and clothes and hairstyles, the latest movies, the latest pop records. She switched to Apia and a stream of the latest gossip: the stream was filled with skeletons and rotting corpses and insects and unmentionable creatures he didn't know or want to have identified for him. Of course

197

she and her family played no part in any of this, she ended that part of her narrative.

Her father was very religious and was a high-up overseer in the best private firm in town, she said. Her mother spoke fluent English. All her family were part-Europeans who had little patience with the fa'a-Samoa. Her father held a very high matai title, she added. But her father and all her uncles and aunts had told her that there was nothing worth knowing about the fa'a-Samoa; all Samoans were dishonest bludgers without any education at all. The palagi way of life was much better, she said.

As she talked, he observed her closely. She exuded a rich aura of sexuality; her body was full and lush. This was her real truth. He suddenly felt a strong need to touch that truth, shatter the flimsy facade of sophistication, and, for a complete moment, live in the truth of her flesh, stripped clean of that artificial, tragic mimicry.

He asked her if she wanted to go to the pictures with him.

'I'd love to. But are you sure you want to take me out?' she said.

He avoided touching her in any way during the film. He was afraid that any contact before he took her back to his room would turn his need for her into revulsion. When they left the theatre, he sensed that he didn't need to persuade her to come to his room. He knew that to her they were a palagi couple to whom Samoan mores didn't apply. A palagi woman was free to do whatever she wanted to.

Most of the lights in the hotel lobby were out. As they went in she told him they didn't need to worry about her parents. She had phoned and told them that she had a lot of work to do and would have to sleep at the hotel. He asked her if she had done this often before. She insisted she hadn't, ever.

She moved into his side as they went up the stairs. He put his arm round her waist and caressed her hip. He looked down at her. Her eyes were half closed.

Once in the room, with the bedside lamp casting a flimsy, eerie light on the floral bedcover, she shifted into his arms, face nuzzling wildly into his chest, lips searching through his shirt for his bare flesh, then teeth nipping and sending veins of enthralling pain down his spine into his loins. She moaned softly.

'I love you,' she murmured as he started to unzip her dress. 'I love you.' The heat drained from him. He eased her away and, holding her at arm's length, studied her face. She blinked and was out of the spell.

Looking round the room, she said, 'How did we get here?'

As he walked over to the bed, he peeled off his shirt and dropped it on the floor. She turned her back when he took off his lavalava. 'I shouldn't be here, should I?' she said. 'I'd better go home.' But she made no move to leave.

'Turn round,' he said.

She turned slowly. Gasped. Shut her eyes when she saw he was naked. 'You shouldn't have done that,' she said.

He drew her against him. 'Why not?' he asked. She shivered in his arms.

'What we're going to do is bad,' she whispered in Samoan. 'It's sinful!' she murmured as he caressed her shuddering flanks.

He stretched her out on the bed. She forgot herself completely under him, her hands clutching the headboard of the bed, her head flung back. She writhed slowly. A purring torrent of words — a language all her own — issued from her quivering mouth.

'I love you!' she moaned as he thrust into her.

She thrashed from side to side, as though all her bones and flesh and mind were melting into one whirling ball of fire. He observed her every reaction. Her voice grew hoarse, and the unintelligible river of moaning and words raged louder; uncontrollable currents forced her body to heave up and down wildly, tightly, buckling and straightening; her mouth sucked in ragged gasps of air and released them in sobs, as she soared up into the stunning light of a moon which only she could see and be guided by. She cried out repeatedly, and he knew she was ready to break, fall back again into the coldness of the earth and what she had become.

He stopped. Held her tightly.

'No!' she cried. 'Please!'

'Do you love me?' he whispered.

'Yes, yes, I love you. Please!'

He gripped her hair and pulled down. 'Tell me the truth!'

Tears streamed from the corners of her closed eyes; she pummelled feebly at his back with her fists. 'You can't leave me like this!'

'It's not a sin, is it?'

'No!'

'You like it, don't you?'

'Yes!'

'And you don't love me and I don't love you?' he asked. She tried to move her hips against him. He pinned her down with his full weight. 'Okay, I don't love you!' she confessed. 'Now, please ...!' He resumed the rhythmic movement of his hips. 'Good,' she murmured. 'Good!'

Her eyes opened for the first time, and in their wild, vulnerable stare he saw the light of the room webbed there like a permanent cloud of gold. She uttered her release into the emptiness above his head.

For that eternal instant when he came, the image of the other girl dazzled his eyes. She had killed their child, and he had helped her. That crime would separate them for ever.

The receptionist visited him in his room whenever she was free. Sometimes she spent the whole night with him. After a week he could no longer bear the daytime town — the whirling dust and dirt, the noisy heat, the endless bustle of crowds and traffic. So he spent much of the day in the library or in his room. At night the town was a sedate mausoleum of muted light and silence afloat on the purring sea. He liked that.

The more he came to know the town and the receptionist the less he could separate them in his mind: she was the town, and there was nothing permanently real and meaningful beyond what he fed on to try to defeat his loneliness, his yearning for the other girl. He hated himself for using her, but every time she touched him his body raged with desire and he made love to her. She seemed to welcome it. But even the sexual fantasies he enacted with her couldn't heal him.

Near the end of his stay in Apia, he realised that, if he worked there, he would find it almost impossible to be happy, for the town was more an overgrown obese village than a city, incestuously feeding on its inhabitants and turning them into shadows of its own image.

One night as they lay on the bed, she began to cry into her pillow. He asked her what was wrong. She was a bad girl, she said in Samoan. She was leading a sinful life with him and she was afraid to go to confession. Sorrow gave way to abandoned panting and a heaving body as soon as he began to make love to her; and, as they attacked each other, she described in moaning pornographic detail what he was doing to her and what she wanted him to make her do.

Afterwards she suggested that they should get married. Then she wouldn't feel sinful any more. They could go to New Zealand. She would make him a good wife because she really loved him. She knew she hadn't had much education, but she could attend night school or he could teach her. He got off the bed. She loved him, she said.

He went out on to the veranda and watched the darkness crouching over the harbour and the town, its furred back bristling against the stars. She came after him and reached out to embrace him.

'Don't touch me,' he said.

37

The day after he returned to the village he told his father what he was going to do. His father's immediate reaction was unexpected: he simply glanced at him, nodded, and didn't refer to it again for three days, while they finished painting the outside of their new house. He didn't tell the others either. Then, after Sunday dinner, while the rest of the family slept, his father asked him to come with him. He wasn't surprised when his father started to walk into the family plantation.

It hadn't rained for nearly two weeks, and the vegetation drooped in the relentless heat. The carpet of leaves under the trees was bone dry; it crackled and snapped under their feet. As they drew away from the village, the silence deepened, filling their ears like warm wax.

When they reached the palm grove they stopped at the rim of the circle, under one of the trees. Surprised that someone had cleared the grave, his father glanced at him. He nodded.

'So you knew all along where he was buried?' his father asked.

'I just guessed,' he said.

'I thought I was going to surprise you.'

His father walked over to the grave and stood above it, his shadow protecting it from the sun. The cleared ground surrounding the grave was parched dry and criss-crossed with cracks. In the brilliant light his father appeared as if he was a permanent part of the grove, an essential piece of its design.

'Nearly forty years now,' his father said. 'In all that time I couldn't forget him, even when I tried to. It was like trying to forget where you began, your whole past. Like trying to obliterate your conscience.' He returned to the shade and sat down on the boulder near his son.

'Did he want to be buried here?' he asked his father.

'Who else would want to be buried away from every other human being?'

He wanted his father to go on unravelling the final meaning of his grandfather's life, but he didn't. He just sat gazing at the grave for a long time. Mosquitoes stung at the silence while he waited and listened to his father's breathing. Through the heads of the trees to the south, the mountain range rose up blue and high and insurmountable.

Chuckling unexpectedly, his father clapped his hands, and said in English: '*He was a weird bugger!*' For a moment he couldn't believe what he had heard. His father's very New Zealand remark seemed so incongruous, but it was — so he would later conclude — a most apt description of his grandfather. His father looked across at him and, smiling deeply, said in Samoan: 'A strange fellow but you would have liked him and he would have loved you most out of all those he called "his spineless descendants".' His father paused. He felt uncomfortable under his scrutiny. 'You look like him too. You've always reminded me of him. Even more so now that I've watched you trying to live in Samoa. But I've never told you that before, have I? Why?' He paused again . . . . 'Because, even though I loved him and admired him and thought him a very courageous man, I didn't really want you to turn out like him. True, I wanted you to be a doctor, a healer, like him. But I didn't want you to be like him as a man.' He sighed and looked at the bare ground. 'Aren't you going to ask me why? . . . I think you know already,' he added slowly.

'Why?' he insisted. He had to hear it from his father.

Looking steadily at him, his father said: 'Because he saw too clearly, too honestly. Do you know what I mean?'

'Yes,' he admitted, and somehow the heat began to weigh lightly on his body.

'Like him you see too clearly. And, because of that, like him you will never be happy with things as they are. Like him you will always be in permanent exile. You will never belong anywhere.' Before he could answer, his father got up and went towards the grave. Over the years many of the stones and rocks had rolled off the tiers. His father started to pick them up and place them carefully back on the grave. He went and helped him.

As they worked, his father continued talking. The sun beat down on them. 'As a child I always envied him,' his father said. 'During the time in New Zealand I continued to envy him. He was a free man; he didn't seem to need anybody else. I envied him until I saw what was happening to you. In exile you acquired the gift that he had — the gift, the curse, that stops you from belonging to anybody or anything. To belong, to feel really needed, you would have to destroy the very gift which keeps you strong, free, separate from us weaker, more human, human beings.' He stopped and slapped at a mosquito on his shoulder. 'I envy you, I love you as my favourite son, but I feel sorry for you. And I blame myself for it. I blame your mother as well. We shouldn't have taken you away from here. We shouldn't have tried to live our hopes, dreams, pretensions, and lives through you and your brother. And especially through you, for your brother is safe. He is content with what he is; he accepts things for what they are.' He wiped the sweat off his face with the corner of his lavalava. 'I always regretted the fact that your grandfather died before I could acquire the secrets of his cures, the gift of what he was as a man. I don't regret that any more. I'm at least satisfied with what I am. I'm happy in Samoa now. At least, I *feel* I am happy here and will not feel incomplete as a man even if you leave us and go back to New Zealand. You were always a crutch for me and your mother. We used you to prop up our pride, our hopes, with your accomplishments and grace and beauty and courage. We returned to Samoa and you were going to give us status, class, in the eyes of our friends, village, country. I know that now, and feel free by admitting it to myself. Now I can live quietly in Samoa and my life will end quietly. Samoa is a beautiful place for the purpose. I'm content with that.' He reached over and placed a warm hand on his son's shoulder. 'You owe me nothing. But the debt I owe you I can never repay. Try to belong to something, someone, even God. Even your grandfather belonged to something: he belonged to the past. He really died before he was born. He couldn't live in the present though he tried to after he married your grandmother.' He stopped suddenly as if he had inadvertently revealed a terrible secret which he shouldn't have. 'It's really hot, isn't it?' his father said, to try to distract him, staggering up, stretching his arms and yawning loudly, and moving back into the shade of the palm tree.

A short time later, when he had placed the last stone back on the grave, he joined his father in the shade. His father lay on his back on the carpet of creepers, his eyes closed as if he was asleep.

His shirt was wet with sweat, so he stripped it off, wiped his face and body with it, and spread it out on the boulder to dry. As the sweat dried he felt cooler. He sat opposite his father and watched him. Mosquitoes settled on him and started sucking his blood, but he didn't notice them.

'He killed her, didn't he?' he asked.

His father's eyes blinked open. 'Who?' And he shut his eyes again and folded his arms across his chest.

'You know who I mean,' he said emphatically.

His father slapped at a fat mosquito on his cheek and squashed it into a small red dot. 'I don't want to talk about it,' he said.

'So it is true.'

'What is true?' His father sat up and looked at him.

He looked away and said: 'That he killed her.'

'Who the hell you talking about?' his father asked in English.

'Grandfather,' he said. That one word seemed to hit his father like a heavy physical blow. He shut his eyes tightly and shook his head; his body twitched as if a fever was coursing through his veins. 'Who told you that?' he said.

'Are you all right?' he asked. He reached over to touch his father but he pushed his hand away.

'Who told you that?' his father repeated. 'Someone must have told you.'

He now regretted having asked him. 'Forget it,' he said.

His father sprang to his feet, fists clenched, eyes brimming with tears. 'You had to do it, didn't you? You had to do it. I buried it all inside my guts. I forgot it. And you had to be the one to dig it up again. You. It had to be you. Why? Couldn't you have left the truth alone for this once, for my sake?'

'I'm — I'm sorry,' was all he could say.

Turning his back, his father wept into the swirling silence, releasing his sorrow and pain and anger into the circle, until, composed again, he sat down and gazed into his shadow.

'Like him you have to know the truth always, don't you?' he said after a long silence. 'He would pick at it until the sores opened and blood spurted out. Pick at it, pick at it, until you couldn't hide any more behind the bandage of lies and half-truths; until you were a whimpering, naked wound of pain. But then he would always heal you again by loving you more intensely. And he could love more than anyone else because he could see clearly into you, even into the secret dark corners of your fears.' He was talking more to himself than to his son; it was a confession, an attempt to expiate the guilt, lift from himself the self-imposed curse. 'They said he was a pagan, a savage, a witch-doctor who loved the dark and the demons who inhabited that darkness. As I grew up I started to believe them, and I denied him in my own heart. Yes, he was a pagan, and he loved the darkness because he understood it. And he wasn't a savage. How could he have been a savage when he was capable of so much love? Yes, out of all of us, he was the most civilised. I admit that now. He was truly a healer.' He paused for a moment. . . . 'Have you worked out yet why he planted palms in the form of a circle, and why he chose to be buried here?'

'No,' said his son.

'Life is a circle,' his father explained. 'He believed that the circle of life has no beginning and no end. And that each living thing, even the gods, is part of that circle, part of its centre. He never told me that, but I know it now.'

'Did he believe that right to the end?'

'Yes, I think so.'

'But you're not sure?'

His father shook his head and said, 'No, I'm not sure.'

'But why?' he asked, as fear clutched at his breath.

Turning to gaze at him, his father said; 'Because he *did* kill her. He destroyed the person he had made the centre of the circle of his life.'

His son shook his head furiously. 'No!' he said. 'No, it isn't true!'

'You know it's true,' his father said. 'All you've got to do is admit it to yourself. I have now.' He stood up and, surveying the palm grove and the sky and the grave, said: 'He was a good man. And I will always treasure his memory and will always want to be like him, like you. It's too late now. But it doesn't matter any more. He is still here because these islands are still here. As a boy, he was these islands for me. He was alive and growing, solid and rich, like the earth of this land.' Looking at his son, he added, 'He is here even more now because you're here. But even if you go away, for me he will always be here.' A smile blossomed across his face. 'The bloody bugger won't leave me alone,' he said in a mixture of English and Samoan. 'And it's bloody good. I accept the bugger now, utterly. Did you know, he could out-fart anyone in the bloody world! Ha! The bloody bugger!'

As he watched his father come alive with joy, he too accepted; the circle had not disintegrated; the centre had held and would continue to hold. The best, like his father, still possessed conviction. And he wanted to go over and embrace him and dance with him on his grandfather's grave.

'I think you're very much like him,' he called to his father, who was now sitting on the grave.

'What?' his father said.

'I said you must be like him.'

'No!' his father replied. 'I'm not as tough; not as civilised. Not as virile!' And they laughed together.

His father came and sat down beside him again. 'I feel free now. Free. I forgive him. And I didn't fail him. Even if I did, I don't care any more. Anyway I didn't really fail him; now he has you, even though you're so palagi!' He ruffled his son's hair. 'Are you ready for the whole truth now?' his father asked a little while later. His son nodded. His father told him.

He married her when she was only eighteen. They were together for nearly thirty years. They had four sons. She died at the age of forty-seven, when she was pregnant for the fifth time and he was about sixty-five years old. There were whispered rumours that he had killed her.

Eight years later he died unexpectedly — no one knows to this day the cause of his death. The night before he died he confessed to his youngest son, who was then ten years old, that he had performed an abortion on her in complete secrecy. This had killed her. The child was not his, he had believed. He was wrong. He knew this when the operation proved unsuccessful and he tried in vain to save her. In desperation, he even took her to the palagi doctors in the town hospital but her life continued to bleed away into a cold, unforgiving silence.

Doubting her love for the first time, he had misused his only real gift and skill, and he had paid for it, he confessed. He had betrayed his whole past; he had betrayed the only person he had ever really loved; and he had betrayed himself.

Perhaps it was because he had loved her too completely when he had not fully conquered his own fears and shadows and vanity as a man. We forget too easily what we are, and — most of all — the beauty we are capable of if we heal ourselves. There are no evil spirits or wrathful gods; we are, in the final instance, not victims of circumstance either. We are all equal in our affliction and our guilt. We secrete the poison of that affliction. The cure is love, he said finally.

He had wanted his favourite son to forgive him. His son was too young then to understand fully.

You've lost her, haven't you?
  Yes.
And you blame yourself?
  Yes.
Are you going back because you want to find her again?
  No.
But why then?
  I don't really know.
Funny, but I miss New Zealand too. I miss that factory and that machine I worked with and lived with for nearly twenty years. Funny how we come to love things that are so inhuman, isn't it. Even now I love the feel and smell of plastic, steel, iron, concrete . . . . I miss that ugly, cruel city, with its insatiable roots stabbed into the earth, choking it; breathing all its poisons into the sky; its blood contaminating the people and turning them against one another in perpetual combat which no one ever wins. And I will always miss that fat man, the first friend I ever made in New Zealand. And then betrayed.

38

The house was completed; the water tank and electric generator were working faultlessly; their furniture, which had arrived in huge crates from New Zealand months before, was unpacked and placed in the house; but as yet they had not moved in. His mother however had already laid down certain rules to the whole family about the occupancy and use of the house. Apart from her and her husband and sons, only his one remaining uncle and his wife were to sleep in the house; the rest of the family had to continue to use the three family fale. All the ordinary family meals were to be cooked in the communal kitchen fale and eaten in the main fale; the shiny kitchen and dining room of the new house were to be used only for special meals for overseas visitors or important people from the town, who, she explained, were used to such amenities. Similarly, the use of the flush toilet was to be confined to the elders, important guests, and the pastor and his wife. The stove, fridge, toaster, cake-mixer, sewing machine, and other electrical appliances were to be operated only by her (and the women she was going to train). Apart from the chosen few, no other member of the family, especially the children, was to be in the house at any time without her permission. It took a long time and much training and care to get used to a palagi house, she explained. She promised to supervise this training. The members of the village who had not been chosen to use the house were very eager to be invited to it because, though many of them now had palagi houses, built with money sent by their relatives in

New Zealand, this was the most expensive and marvellous house of all, with its electric lights and appliances, its internal water-tap system and flush toilet, its padded armchairs and settees, its mahogany furniture and cupboards, its coffee tables and glass cabinet, its innerspring mattresses, its unbelievable collection of family portraits and coloured photographs of New Zealand, its trophies, its screen wiring to keep out insects, its red and white tiled floors, its walls of dazzling reds and pinks and blues, its large oak-panelled gramophone and radio and its library of long-playing records, its sitting-room wall lined with bookshelves full of the largest number of books they would ever see in a lifetime, and its television set which they heard was to be installed soon. This was a genuine palagi house, like the houses their relatives in New Zealand lived in; this was also the kind of house owned by wealthy Samoans in the town. (And they all aspired to such status.) The few dissenters in the village, mainly his mother's enemies, accused them publicly of being nobodies trying to be somebodies. But they too were secretly manoeuvring to regain her friendship and thereby gain access to her house.

He found his mother in the kitchen of the new house. Stopping in the doorway, he watched her as she cleaned the cupboards and stacked crockery in them. She had put on more weight; she made the kitchen look small. She sensed his presence, turned, and asked him where he had been. He told her he had been out in the plantation getting taro, bananas, and firewood. She continued working while he watched her.

The invigorating breeze blowing in through the louvre windows could not dispel the tenacious smell of fresh paint. Outside, the sand on the ground was blind with blazing sun. Some of the children he had been to the plantation with came and stood at the windows and peered into the room. His mother asked two of the oldest girls to come in and help her; they entered timidly through the back door. She showed them what to do, and then sat down on one of the dining chairs to rest for a while.

The children outside started to scribble with their fingers in the dust which coated the screens; she ordered them to go away. They giggled and ducked down out of sight, but they could be heard whispering among themselves. A dog barked from behind the house. He saw a pig scrambling frantically past the window. He walked into the dining room, stopped, turned to leave again.

'What's the matter with you?' she asked in Samoan.

He shrugged his shoulders. 'Nothing,' he said.

A saucepan clanged loudly on the concrete floor. One of the girls had dropped it. His mother told her to be more careful; money doesn't grow on trees, she said. His mother winked at him. 'Boy, it hot, isn't it?' she said in English. (She spoke with a very nasal New Zealand accent.) 'Sure wish we was back in New Zealand. It really cool dere.' He looked away, trying not to laugh. In New Zealand she had rarely spoken English in their home, but now in Samoa she used every available opportunity to impress the villagers with her English. 'Dese people got lot to learn 'bout cleaning a house prop'ly. Dey so dirty in deir habits,' she said, looking at the girls. 'New Zealand is a clean place — clean shops, houses, streets. Boy, I sick of dirt here!'

The new house was to be her sanctuary from the heat and dirt and insects, he thought; her symbol of high status and sophistication and civilisation; her badge of honour, which she knew was envied by every mother in the village and which she could use to gain the leadership over all the other women. A New Zealand oasis in the middle of the wilderness, earned by over twenty years in exile. She had even wanted air-conditioning for the house but they had opposed her.

'You miss New Zealand?' he asked.

She shook her head. 'Not really,' she said. 'I happy here.'

'But you miss some things?'

Without answering him, she got up and started working again with the girls.

He went to have a shower.

212

Half an hour later, his skin still tingling from the cold spray of the shower, he returned to the dining room.

She was sitting in an armchair, gazing out through the louvre windows. The girls were gone; so were the children. She asked him to sit down beside her. 'You want lunch?' she asked in English. He shook his head. Through the windows they could see the rest of the family having their midday meal in the main fale. The breeze had died away, and the ti plants, sugarcane, and palm trees round the fale were dead still, as if in a photograph.

'You happy here?' she asked in Samoan.

'Yes,' he replied, 'I'm happy here.'

Looking at him, she said, 'I'm glad. I knew you'd love it here.'

She paused. 'I love it here,' she added. 'Of course I do miss our old home now and then.'

'But this is your home,' he said, testing her.

She laughed. 'Yes, I meant our other home in New Zealand.'

He hesitated for a moment. 'I'm happy here, Mamma,' he began in English, 'but . . . . ' He could feel her staring at him.

'But what?' she asked.

He got up, walked slowly to the windows, and, with his back to her, said, 'But I don't think I can live here.'

'That doesn't make sense to me,' she said quickly. 'If you're happy in a place you can live in that place.'

He turned to look at her. She looked away. 'I can't,' he said, watching her closely, expecting a bitter outburst, dramatic disappointment. But she simply bowed her head.

'What are you going to do then?' she asked, as if she had already accepted his departure.

'I don't want to hurt you,' he said.

She shook her head. 'You're not hurting me,' she said.

He believed her. 'Maybe go back to New Zealand,' he said.

'Back to her?' she asked immediately. He turned away. 'Back to her?' she repeated.

'No,' he said.

213

'But it must be,' she insisted. She would never understand; it was better for him just to go and not try to make her understand.

He wheeled to leave the room. She loomed up out of her chair and blocked his way.

'Please,' he pleaded. 'I don't want an argument.'

She let him go until he reached the door; then she said slowly: *'She can't come back to you anyway.'*

It was as if the whole planet had stopped spinning for that one instant, for that one step that would have taken him through the doorway into the stunning sun and in sight of the boundless horizon.

'What do you mean?' he asked, his back still turned to her. There was only accusing silence. He wheeled and confronted her. 'What do you mean?' he repeated.

She seemed to fill the whole room. She would never give way. 'You know what I mean,' she said.

He had not told anyone what had happened to the girl.

'So you knew all along?' He tried to smother his anger.

'Yes!' she snapped.

He had her; now she wouldn't be able to hide.

'She came to you before she decided to go away?' he asked. She started to tremble, realising what she had done. She turned away from him.

'Didn't she?' he shouted.

'I don't want to talk about it,' she said. 'And you have no right to speak to your mother this way. No son has that right.' She sought refuge behind that one sacred taboo between parents and their children: parents had to be respected, obeyed, served, regardless of how good or evil they were. For a Samoan son to break that code of behaviour would condenm him to exile within his own home, village, community, and country. A mother's curse would destroy a son with guilt, brand him as Cain. He knew this; he also knew that this was now the only right way for him to break away from her and the safety of home and country, and to be what he was. She started to weep.

Most of the family and their neighbours had by now crowded to the windows and were watching them.

214

The back door opened. His brother came into the room. She rushed over to him. 'What's the matter?' his brother asked, holding her. She wept more loudly. His brother sat her down in a chair. 'You can't do this,' his brother cautioned him in English so that the other people wouldn't understand what was going on. 'She's your mother!'

'She is not my mother any more,' he said in Samoan for everyone to hear. The people outside gasped in disbelief and horror, as though they had just heard him declaring for suicide; this was the acceptance of death by a son who had gone mad.

'No!' she wailed.

'He doesn't mean it, Mamma,' his brother said soothingly. 'You don't mean it, do you?' his brother pleaded with him.

Ignoring his brother, he said to her, 'She came to you, didn't she?' She shook her head furiously and beat at her knees with clenched fists. 'Didn't she?' he asked again.

She rose slowly to her feet. 'She killed your child,' she sobbed.

'But you advised her to do it,' he said quietly. Wailing, she shook her head.

He had to do it. He hit her.

The sharp final slap of his forgiving hand across her face broke open the womb of his grief and guilt, and he was free at last.

His brother rushed at him, but their mother hurled herself against him. Stopped him.

39

The plane shuddered with the tremendous strain as it fought against the weight of the falling sky; rising, rising, until it attained that point of balance between the forces pulling it down and those dragging it upwards; then it levelled out.

He unfastened his seat belt; he no longer felt any sensation of motion; it was as if the plane was now fixed forever in a placid timeless sea between his past and his future, and he had nothing to lose. He lay back in his seat. He didn't know why he was going back, but even that didn't seem important any longer.

All round him were people migrating to New Zealand. Silently they sat, trying to overcome their fears of the present — of the plane exploding into flames and hurtling down into the unforgiving solidity of earth or into the sea, into a horrible oblivion. And more distressing fears of what lay ahead — of the wilderness of cold unknown cities in a country which, they had heard, God had forsaken.

But, as the plane continued to defeat fate, to maintain a haughty equilibrium above the chasm below struggling to suck it down, the promise of the future and their dreams of lucrative jobs, money, houses, cars, a good education for their children, calmed their fears, gave meaning to their journey into what they all believed would be only a temporary exile from which they would return unharmed, unchanged, rich.

His satchel was under the seat. He pulled it up, unzipped

it, and searched through his papers for the seven poems he had written about her.

As he read them she came alive again.

Then he tore up each poem carefully.

He had nothing to regret; nothing to look forward to. All was well. He was alive; at a new beginning. He was free of his dead.

He took out his pen, and on the cover of the slick Technicolor tourist brochure which he found in the plastic bag of airline gifts that the smiling hostess had given him, he wrote in large letters: *'And Hine-nui-te-Po woke up and found him in there. And she crossed her legs and thus ended man's quest for immortality.'*

He imagined Maui to have been happy in his death.

Glossary

alofa (Samoan),
aroha (Maori) love, compassion; a present, a gift

ava or kava ceremonial drink made from roots of ava 'or kava' plant

fa'a Samoa the Samoan way of doing things, the Samoan way of life

fale Samoan house

lavalava skirt-like wrap-around garment

luau taro leaves cooked with coconut cream

matai titled head of a family

palagi or papalagi person of European stock

pandanus plant whose leaves are used for making mats

siva to dance (v.), a Samoan dance (n.)

taro (Maori),
talo (Samoan) a plant the bulbous root of which is cooked and eaten

ti a plant sometimes used for medicinal purposes

umu stone oven